LA MADONNA NEGRA | VOLUME I

"Violent and twisted."

"Cinematic and visually sumptuous."

Enter the mysterious world of La Madonna Negra!

She never dreamed.

Until the nightmares started.

Forced to flee the scene and the only home she ever knew, Yael finds herself in the shadows of the Ybor slums. For years she hid the truth from those around her, wearing her smile like a mask as she spiraled into the abyss.

With her whole life behind her, she has no need for hopes and dreams. Alone and beyond broken, she chases her nightmares to avoid her grim reality. So when she finally sees the chance to join the living, she can't help but question if it really is the light at the end of the tunnel? After all, the last time she was this close to freedom, she lost herself.

Is redemption near? Will the terrifying curse that stole her innocence be lifted if she follows the light? Or will her double life catch up with her in the bitter end?

Find the FIRST book in the adventure series at your local retailer!

LA MADONNA NEGRA

VOLUME II

GRACE FIERY

WELCOME BACK

WE ARE HAPPY

YOU ARE HERE

AUGUST

CHAPTER ONE

Ybor City, FL | 2010

Yael couldn't remember the last time she dreamed. She sat on the edge of her bed and reached over to pull her journal from its hiding place under the alarm clock. Thumbing through the pages of her small black moleskin notebook, she scanned the titles in search of her next victim. It felt like forever since she killed a man, and she *knew* she was past due.

Tapping the tip of her nose with her index finger, she tried to recall her last dream. Each time she had visions in the night, she was shown scattered pieces of a puzzle; the scribbled memories and keywords on these pages would allow her to put things together. The most important clues she received were not about the mark or the weapon, but the *timing*. Every page was titled with a timestamp; the title of every page she turned today was crossed out.

Weird.

Yes, it was odd. She had three years worth of notebooks packed away in the attic above, and this one would soon join them with so few blank pages remaining. The dreams came in their own time, the puzzle pieces slipping into her mind at a steady rate as they helped her paint a picture.

Yael's mind had been clearer as of late; still, she couldn't remember a time where she had a clean queue. Of course, she wasn't complaining. She just knew better than to ignore her calling — bad things happened to good people when she did.

Maybe it's the calm before the storm?

Now, why would you think that? she scolded accusingly.

I'm just anxious. This is anxiety.

Yes! Anxiety. That was all.

Ever since she started reading Joe's psychology books last week, she was finding it easier to stop herself from what she called 'anxious spiraling'. Old anxiety had led to five years of depression. Though she had good reason to be depressed back then, she owed it to herself to adjust to life in the light and heal the defects of her mind.

She was going to need all the help she could get, too. When Ricardo offered her the 'day manager' position at Margarita's, she was so out of touch that she misunderstood the role. Last night, he called to ask if she was excited to take over. She wasn't the bar manager or the shift manager, she was the General Manager! Of the whole restaurant! She'd been anxious ever since.

It *was* a little exciting, though.

When she and Joe finally had their next 'get to know you' discussion, she would have a job description she could be proud of. Not that she felt he would judge her for working as a bartender — he was far too kind to care about that sort of thing. But she did care. She wanted to impress him and this would be a good place to start.

2

Her phone buzzed on the dresser behind her. Tossing the notebook down and placing her mother's pen onto the nightstand, she tumbled backward on the bed and rolled onto her feet.

"Joe," she whispered, smiling broadly as she read his text.

Even though they were still only on a first name basis, Yael felt like she'd known him her whole life. She understood that the honeymoon was over, but she hated being apart from him for even a few hours. Sitting in the peaceful silence of his presence was like nothing she'd ever experienced. Knowing he missed her even though they'd spent the morning and most of the last two weeks together warmed her to the core.

"Missing you," she breathed through her smile as she replied to his SMS message. "See…you…later."

Tossing her phone onto the bed and whirling around like a Disney princess, she let out a gleeful sigh that turned into a squeal of excitement. Catching herself in the mirror, she winked and shot finger guns at her beaming reflection.

She was positively radiant, glowing vibrantly in her grey velour shorts and orange Guavaween t-shirt. If she didn't know any better, she would say she was pregnant. At least that's what she'd heard people say to women who looked as happy as she felt. There was no way she could be, still being a damned virgin, but maybe she was giving birth to something else…

Eating well all week had thickened her torso, but she could still see the curved lines of her abs when she lifted her shirt. Toned and visibly strong from years of training her body at the dojo, there was no doubt she worked out. She was also what her mother had termed 'hippy'. Wide hips, muscular quads, and large, toned calves were in perfect proportion to her big, round bottom. Taking after her mother in almost every trait, she was slightly taller than average and lugged around full breasts that often got in her way. But where her mother's skin was a deep, rich pecan, her father's Italian & Sicilian blood had given Yael's skin a tone between peanut butter and golden honey.

Yael smiled and laughed more in the last month than she had in the five years that she lived here at the manor. A decade had likely passed since she felt this kind of joy, because the last time she remembered feeling so full of life was when her mother was alive.

I wonder if mom would have liked Joe?

A tinge of sadness threatened to burst her bubble. She pushed the thought from her mind, instead making a mental note to apply for a library card so she could read about the psychology of mourning. Her father never allowed her to mourn anyone and she didn't know the first place to start. All Yael knew was she wanted to stay happy — for Joe.

It wasn't that she loved him — it was too soon for *all that* — she just wanted to reprogram her brain. She didn't want the pain of her past to become a recurring issue. She didn't want her inability to cope with the dark side of her life to impact her time with him in the light. She didn't want any of the stains of this curse to blacken Joe's heart of gold. All she wanted was to make him happy, and she'd never wanted anything more than this.

Before Joe came from heaven and landed in her life, she was a dead woman walking on a path to hell. Her ex-boyfriend — ex-fiancee? — was now the *He-Who-Must-Not-Be-Named* of her past, and with good reason. It wasn't that he was a lying, cheating, drug lord who tricked her into drinking Rohypnol each time they shared an intimate moment. It wasn't that he was partly the reason she got caught up with the mafia. And it wasn't that he intended on making her his possession, his sex slave for life through their 'marriage contract'…

Xavier Duke Hill was the man who killed Joe's wife and son. And if Joe ever found out that she and Xavier were together...

She shook off the sinking feeling creeping into her belly. Every moment that passed was another moment she betrayed Joe with this lie. No, she had yet to *outright lie* to Joe without good reason, but lying through omission was just as bad. Maybe worse.

When Xavier went to jail months ago, she didn't realize she'd been living her life of darkness with one foot in and one foot out the door. Now she was being blinded by the light of Joe's love and questioning her ability to maintain her balance at all.

In the time it took her to clear away her old life and embrace the new, so much had changed for the better. To know Xavier was dead? It was almost too good to be true. Though she had her suspicions about all these sudden changes, she had to admit her eyes were finally starting to adjust to being shoved into the dazzling light of day.

All she could do now was hope.

And have faith?

Yes, faith and hope. These would be a nice change from *fear* and *doubt*, which she was still full of. She just needed to learn to be patient with herself.

Opening her bedroom door and heading to check the laundry, she pictured her wardrobe and tried to imagine herself dressed as a GM. Ricardo was the closest thing Margarita's ever had to a manager; as the owner, he wore jeans and polos most days. Hoping she could find something suitable, she forced the doubts from her mind and focused on her plan to get to work on time.

YAEL LAUGHED as she shut her bedroom door. There was a party downstairs, and it wasn't even noon!

Every summer, her cousin Frederico and his best friend PJ pre-ordered the new *Madden* football game. Every year in August, they lined up at the local gaming shop to grab their copy at midnight. If she had known that last night was *the night*, she would have planned to stay at Joe's all week.

I might as well move in now, she mused.

She and Joe were supposed to be taking things slow, yet this was the third time today she'd thought of a good reason to see him as soon as possible. Still, she knew better; they did need to slow down, and moving in was out of the question.

Besides, she and Fred had only recently reconnected after the Xavier fiasco caused a rift between them. She was happy things were (for the most part) back to normal and hoped that as Joe returned to work, she would have a chance to spend family time with Frederico again soon.

Yael jumped at the sudden burst of shouting, then rolled her eyes and stared at the ceiling when the subsequent argument followed. There were at least a dozen young men in her living room right now, all losing their minds over a fake football game. She shook her head and sighed.

"Shit!"

Dropping the laundry basket to the floor, she dove onto the bed to retrieve her dream journal. Carefully clipping her mother's pen to the cover of the notebook, she slid both back into their hiding place on the nightstand.

Frederico never let anyone upstairs after she moved in. Most of the notes were cryptic scribbles. But the timestamps — combined with murder weapons and physical descriptions of her marks —

were probably enough to convict her if anyone figured out the system.

Johhny, her mafia handler, would likely call soon with another job to do. If she didn't have a dream before then, she would have to tell him no again. Yael always had trouble declining his offers to kill marks who weren't in her notebook. Johhny had no idea how she chose her jobs and didn't understand that she wouldn't know what to do without her dreams. She refused to go in blind, knowing she'd be killed or worse, so she dealt with his snippy attitude the best she could.

Yael always wondered if his frustration stemmed from his boss, the Don. She could imagine both men finding her peculiar process irritating, but the Don looked like he had a real temper. Disappointing Johhny probably meant pissing off the Don, and she wasn't at all curious to find out what the man was like when he was angry.

Opening her bedroom door, she walked across the landing to set up the ironing board next to the bathroom. Plugging in the iron, she headed into her room to sift through the basket of mostly black clothes in the hopes she owned a polo shirt she'd forgotten about. She found a black button-down she hadn't worn in months and stepped over to her closet to pick out a pair of dark jeans.

Holding the pants and shirt to her, she studied herself in the mirror. It was a *cute* outfit, though not exactly her style for work. For now, it would have to do until she could find something else — if she went that far. In truth, she knew it wouldn't be long before jeans and a black v-neck became the GM uniform at Margarita's. Casual was always welcome on the Ybor Strip.

Although, she did have work to do *under* Ybor after her shift at Margarita's ended this afternoon. Maybe a new look would show

Johhny she was taking her promotion at the underground bar seriously?

She thought of Johhny, Ricardo, Frederico, and Joe...all the men she answered to as of today. What was once a double life was becoming a quadruple life; she wasn't sure she could handle it, but she did intend to try.

Promise?

She met her eyes in the mirror, then gave a firm nod.

I promise. For Joe.

Yes, if she wasn't going to try for herself, she would at least try for him. And she was going to have to do it right, because Joe was a very observant man. She could only hope that his work kept him busy — so busy, he wouldn't notice her sneaking about.

He's not stupid, you know.

Stop it! Deep breaths.

She inhaled for ten seconds, then held her breath for another ten, trying not to focus on her fears. They would have to get to know each other — as soon as work would allow.

Joe was preoccupied all weekend, obviously nervous about his first day back. Lately, Yael wondered if he was an accountant — or maybe a realtor, with a house so big and much talk of other properties. Was accounting a hard job? Or would real estate do better to keep him on the move? And what about later down the line? How long would his anxiety last?

Was it wrong for her to hope his job was stressful? Not that she wanted her sweet, innocent man under pressure...she just needed...*time.*

With Xavier, she knew she would never have to explain herself. She expected a life with him to make doing her work easy. He didn't seem to care about anything but his dojo and his body.

Joe was different. He was loving and kind. He wanted to *know* her.

Yael simply had to figure out which *her* she would give him.

The bartender turned General Manager at Margarita's?

Or the Ybor vigilante turned hit woman for the local mob?

She didn't know what he would think, but she was sure she didn't have long to find out.

CHAPTER TWO

"Agent Clarke, nice to see you!"

Joe smiled at the chipper woman, her name slipping his mind for a second or two.

"Ms. White, lovely to see you."

"This is your welcome packet," she said quickly, handing him a file as she started down the hall. "They're waiting for you in the conference room."

She paused to point up the steps. Giving him another bubbly smile and two thumbs up, she turned on her heel and walked over to the printer to retrieve a document.

He crossed the floor and hopped up the steps, grinning when he heard the conference room door quickly open and shut. Sighing, he mentally prepared himself for what was about to happen.

"Team? Are you in there?" he asked innocently from outside the door.

A loud snort came from just inside the conference room and he couldn't help but smile. Several audible *shushes* made him laugh out loud. He set a look of shock on his face and swung open the door.

Thunderous applause greeted him.

"Surprise!"

"Welcome back!"

"No. Welcome home," Weaver said with a wink, stepping forward to embrace him.

He hugged her, then put his hands on her shoulders, taking a long look at his old friend.

"Good to be home," he said, giving her an exaggerated wink in return.

"Quit hogging him!"

Joe braced himself when Agent Clancy wedged between them, leaning down to rest his head on Joe's shoulder. At six-foot, seven inches, the gargantuan young Irishman was a force to be reckoned with in the field. At the office, he was a social butterfly who always found someone to assist or converse with about the strangest things. Handsome, rugged, and offputtingly friendly, he had wormed his way into the hearts of the entire agency.

"Where's the cake?"

Joe directed the question to Weaver, knowing Clancy would leap to assist. And assist he did, loudly parting the sea of people to guide Joe to the table across the room.

Joe put his hands up and smiled.

"I know why you're all here."

He sat down and started cutting into the large marble cake as the room erupted in laughter. He wasn't wrong. The Federal Bureau of Investigation was not immune to the doldrums of the workplace; special occasions always involved food, or at the very least, cake. No one was willing to miss cake, especially one with buttercream frosting from the Publix Bakery.

Greeting people as he served them, Joe found himself enjoying his first moments back at work. Nothing ever changed during his FMLA leave. The 'suits' filling the room blended in with the dry, stale vibes of the Westshore FBI office: swaths of beige, navy, steel, and black made it hard to see where the walls ended and the agents began.

When he finally finished, Weaver took over, having been tasked with getting cake to those stuck at their desks. He watched her mumble under her breath as she whipped the cart full of cake slices through the crowd. Waiting to make eye contact, he gave her another wink.

Weaver's face scrunched up, her mouth, nose, and eyes meeting at the center. She stuck out her tongue as she whacked a senior director in the leg on her way out of the conference room.

Joe clapped in delight. It *was* good to be home.

Weaver and Clancy were in Joe's training class when he started at the Bureau, and they had followed him from department to department and team to team all these years. Whereas Clancy was known as the big friendly giant, Weaver might as well be known as the little angry fire ant. Her personality *was* rage and she was always on ten. She was also one of the best agents Joe had ever seen, next to Clancy.

He mingled for a moment, then began searching the room for his boss, Agent Shepherd Boyer. The man was not much for parties. Rolling his eyes, Joe turned to face the door, smirking at Boyer when he found him there.

He raised his eyebrows at Joe and smirked right back. Flashing Joe's badge and firearm, he nodded towards his office.

Joe dropped his head to the side and frowned in protest. He hadn't been expecting to be brought in on a case this soon.

But Boyer's face had turned to stone. Thin lips set in a firm grimace, he shook his head once and walked away. Following him out the door, Joe felt his stomach drop as he recalled the last time he'd seen *that look* in the man's eyes.

Joe remembered like it was yesterday; it was one of the worst cases his team had ever seen. They were on assignment and closing in on a serial murderer. Boyer knocked on the door of his hotel room hours before their wake up call, leading Joe to believe they'd caught the killer.

Instead, Boyer came in, sat him down on the edge of the bed, and gave him the news: as they slept, Joe's wife and son had been killed in a grisly hit-and-run in Tampa. In his numbness and refusal to stop working the case, Joe made more than a few mistakes and almost ruined the arrest. Since that fateful day, he had been placed on leave three separate times — pending psychological evaluation.

Was he fired? Was Boyer about to tell him to go home?

Or was this about his *new* lady love?

Try as he might to force the thoughts from his head, he couldn't help but wonder if something had happened to her since they parted hours earlier.

It's probably about a case. Boyer doesn't even know Yaya.

You never know what the Bureau knows, he countered.

Shaking off the awful images creeping into his mind, he stepped into the office and shut the door behind him.

Boyer was seated at his desk, shuffling files and stacking them into piles. The man wasn't much for words, either, so he and Joe got along well. Each time Boyer was promoted, he promoted Joe into his old position; Weaver and Clancy followed Joe, but Joe followed Boyer.

The only personal information Boyer ever volunteered about himself was that his hair turned grey by the time he was fourteen. He was in his late thirties now, but no one could tell. A stoic nature and uncompromising demeanor combined with his thick grey hair and beard gave Boyer the countenance of an old grump. Weaver liked to spin the tale that Boyer was a lively and free spirited youth, blaming the grey hair for giving the young man a complex. After almost a decade together, Joe was convinced that Boyer's hair turned grey to match his steely personality.

"Welcome back. We've got a case."

"Great," Joe said, his voice thick with sarcasm.

"And you've been promoted."

"Again?"

"Again."

Joe sighed. His last few promotions were really lateral moves in the hierarchy. While the pay and benefits were higher than others in his department, there were also a lot more politics involved for members of the Bureau's upper-middle management — with little to no power to fix anything.

"So I should expect fewer investigations and more bureaucracy?"

Boyer smirked. "What do you want to know first?"

"What do I have to deal with first?"

"We've got a serial, local."

"How local?"

"Tri-city."

"Here in Tampa?"

Boyer opened a case file. "Clairmel, Lakeland, St. Petersburg, and various locations around the city, including South Tampa. In fact, most of the sites are between our office and Brandon."

Joe sat back and sighed. "Do we have a signature?"

"Exsanguination."

Lip curling, Joe shifted uncomfortably in his seat. "How many bodies?"

"Sixteen so far, with the first dating back two years."

"How?" Joe exclaimed.

Boyer frowned in question.

"Sixteen people exsanguinated in two years in *our jurisdiction* and we're just getting the case? I don't get it?"

Nodding, Boyer listed off the pertinent details. "He doesn't always use the blood the same way. Most of the deceased were discovered once there was a smell and more than half of them have ties to the mafia. This office investigated two of these locations, but it wasn't our department."

"Alright," Joe sighed. "And we're sure it's a he?"

"Clancy and Weaver seem to think so, but you'll start fresh. There wasn't a pattern until about six months ago, and it appears he's escalating. You're taking lead while I'm on special assignment."

CHAPTER THREE

Yael woke up to shooting pains in her forehead. She tried opening her eyes, but the pain only grew more intense. Squeezing her eyes shut, she sat up and pressed the butt of her palm into her eyebrows. Movement beside her reminded her she was not alone.

Exhaling softly, she leaned back into the couch. She was at Joe's. Feeling his warmth next to her was soothing, and she found the pain was already subsiding.

What's happening to me?

A flash of red tore through her mind, sending another sharp pain to her forehead. She held her breath, wondering if Joe was watching her writhe in silent agony.

No, he would never just *watch…*

Wait…what am I doing here*?*

Why *was* she here? The last thing she remembered was getting ready for bed at home in her room. Oh, yes! Joe had called her and asked if she'd eaten. She picked up dinner to celebrate his first day back to work.

Why are we on the couch?

If she weren't in pain, she would have smiled. She and Joe were very good at avoiding the end of their time together. And tonight was their first official try at 'taking things slow'; she was supposed to leave but never got around to it.

Another burst of red, this one more vivid, brought her to the brink. This time, she tried to make out the room she was seeing through the fog of her mind.

Shit! She took a deep breath. *Was I dreaming?*

If she had been, she was undoubtedly going about this the wrong way.

When the subsequent flood of red came crashing into her mind, she grabbed ahold of the horrifying feeling and found herself sucked into a clear vision of a day she'd never lived…

She saw a man – and she killed him.

Then she left him there – made a phone call.

But here – where most of her dreams were supposed to end – *Yael saw herself turn around and go back.*

Moving in the shadows, she found a window, watched, and then –

Yael returned to her body with a gasp.

She looked at Joe and found him deep in slumber. The pain was gone as if it had never been. But the memory – the strange vision – was still as clear as day.

Gradually getting to her feet, she walked to the dining room table to retrieve her purse and left the house, locking the bottom knob behind her. Within minutes, she was flying down Gandy Boulevard like a madwoman, cursing her decision to bring only one gun and no extra ammo. She didn't have to go far, but she drove like her life depended on it.

THIRTEEN MINUTES LATER, she came to a screeching halt and jumped out of her car. Running up the driveway, she tapped on the door to the security booth with the barrel of her gun. The guard eyed her warily before opening the sliding door.

"Oh, Ms. Phillips! You frightened me! I-Is everything alright?"

Lifting her gun so he could see it, she sneered, "Take me to him."

"Miss, please! You know I can't -"

Yael popped him one with the butt of her pistol. He stumbled back and fell into his swivel chair. Pointing the weapon at his groin, she leaned in and spoke softly.

"Let's try this again. Take me to him or I shoot the dick off of every man I see. You first."

Tapping his zipper, she cocked her head to the side and waited. He started to reach for his bloody nose but decided against it, lifting his hands instead. He trained his eyes on the gun at his crotch, nodding breathlessly.

Backing up, she allowed him to stand and took the gun from the holster on his belt. Following him out the back door of the security hut with her weapon pressed into his lower back, they used a short footbridge to cross the moat.

The neighborhood was silent — not that it mattered. The encircling high walls gave her all the privacy she needed as they navigated the sprawling lawn that led to the mansion. A hundred feet later, the guard punched a code into a concealed side door. Waiting for a loud beep from the keypad, he swung the door open so they could enter the house, then led her down a hallway and into an opulent living area.

Where the hell are we?

Her first job with the mob had required her to come here, but she was so nervous that night she barely noticed her surroundings.

Another key difference from that evening? She had been *invited* in; she used the front door when she made her way to the office to meet her first mark. Maybe that was why she'd forgotten the mansion was so massive? Why hadn't she considered that he could be leading her into a trap?

"How far is it?" she asked as they turned another corner.

When he didn't answer, she pressed the gun deeper. Her patience was wearing thin, so she gave him a little encouragement.

"I think I can hit both nuts from back here."

"Just up ahead!" he shouted, voice cracking. "The master is right up the stairs."

Son of a -

Yael sucked her teeth and smashed her gun into the back of his head. He dropped to his knees in pain, grasping the new injury with one hand and hovering over his nose with the other. She kicked him down and pointed the gun at him, but he didn't put up a fight. Stepping over him, she kicked him once more for good measure and started towards the stairs.

There was only one door at the top of the steps, so she opened it and slid into the darkness. The room was huge, but all she cared about was the occupant of the giant bed in the center. When she reached the foot of the bed, she climbed onto a long bench and stood to take aim.

Alarm bells suddenly blared throughout the house.

The Don jumped, reaching for the lamp on the side of his bed. Yael pointed both weapons at the man and wife staring up in shock.

The woman fainted.

Yael kept her gun on the woman as she asked the Don, "Why?"

His mouth dropped open in confusion.

"You lied to me!"

He flinched at the sound of her shriek, then shook his head.

"Never," he whispered.

"Tell me his name." Tears were flowing down her cheeks.

The Don blinked. "Who?"

"Tell me his name!" she screamed, the crack in her voice deepening as she lost her temper.

"Who, damn it? Who!" he shouted, still shaking his head.

Yael's face twisted as she tried to find her voice. "He hasn't been cleaning."

The Don's eyes flared, but she barely registered his response as she forced out the words.

"He's been…feeding! Bleeding them like sheep!"

He gasped.

"I told you!"

The shout gave Yael a start.

The sharp-faced blonde with rollers in her hair was now conscious, screeching and slapping her husband with great fury.

"I told you! *Vaffanculo, Sammy*! *Ci sei cascato come una pirla*! I fucking told you not to trust that – that – *porco Guida*!"

The older woman was crying accusingly, as if sensing her fate. It was obvious she hated the man Yael had come here to identify. But what did that tell her?

What was she saying?

'You fell for it?'

'You idiot?'

Did the woman know something the Don did not?

"*Ma, che sei grullo*?" the woman asked, beating his chest and shoulder with both fists.

"Shut her up," Yael snipped, her voice cold. "Now!"

The Don turned to his wife, grabbing her tiny fists in an attempt to stop the pummeling. His eyes moved anxiously between two the women in the room.

"Basta, basta! Basta, Gloria!"

"*Ma, che sei grullo?*"

His wife was sobbing uncontrollably, asking him over and over how he could be so stupid. Pulling her into his side, he covered her mouth and stared up at Yael.

"*Taci!*" Yael cried, growing irritable.

The alarm *stopped*.

The couple looked at the ceiling, then stared at Yael in horror.

She glanced left and right, finding the moment odd herself. Her eyes landed on the door, and for the first time she considered that she might have to shoot her way out. Aiming one gun at the woman's forehead and the other at the door, she looked at the Don and asked again.

"His name?"

He shook his head. "Do you know how dangerous -"

"Do you think I care, old man? He's a fucking monster! He's…"

She shook her head. Stepping backward, she slinked towards the French doors behind her.

"You know what, fine! I'll find him myself!"

She unlocked the door, swinging it wide as she walked out to the balcony to assess her options for escape. When she saw the steps leading down to the pool area, she huffed and shot a grateful glance at the sky before hurrying down the way.

CHAPTER FOUR

The Don shoved Gloria off of him and leaned over to press the intercom on the phone system.

"Get Johhny over here now! Now, damn it!"

Fumbling to open the drawer of his nightstand, he pulled out the walkie talkie and turned it on. Pressing the button, he shouted his orders.

"Cancel the alert and bring her back. And unless you wanna die, don't fucking touch her, you hear me?!"

The voice on the other end answered hesitantly. "*Uhh, copy.*"

"Get your father on the phone," he said harshly as he turned to face his wife. "The Families meet at dawn!"

Climbing out of bed with the walkie in hand, he rushed onto the balcony through the French doors. He could see Yael walking along the edge of the moat. If he remembered correctly, the gators weren't set to be fed for another week. And per protocol, the bridge would still be up.

The Don ran back inside, heading straight to his security closet behind a false wall. Lifting the gold wainscoting until the latch released, he entered the small room and searched. He didn't see her on any of the screens until two of his guards came into view, approaching her slowly with hands raised.

"Fuck."

Matteo and Leonardo were fiercely loyal, having been with him for years. Matteo's fealty knew no bounds. Ordinarily, this wouldn't be a problem, but tonight Matteo's swift form of justice was far more firepower than he needed. Just as the Don's worry turned into panic, he saw Leo motion toward Matteo. They both stopped in their tracks.

"Nice, Leo."

He held his breath as Yael raised both guns and glanced down at the moat. By the looks of things, someone was going to die tonight.

"Don't do it, girl," he muttered.

Clutching his chest, he took a breath as a sharp pain set in under his breastplate.

When Johhny ran into view, the Don slumped into the leather chair behind him in relief. Maybe there was hope for the night after all? As both his *consigliere* and first cousin, Johhny was the only person on the property who could be trusted to bring this to an end without bloodshed.

Eyes jumping from screen to screen, he watched as the cavalry closed in around the night's intruder. Johhny waved his gun in the air, barely able to make it across the lawn as he approached the water's edge.

"Geez, Johhny."

The Don massaged the bridge of his nose. If Johhny didn't get shot tonight, he would be going on a diet in the morning.

CHAPTER FIVE

"D on't – don't shoot! Don't shoot!" Johhny wheezed, holding his robe closed with one hand and waving his gun in the air with the other.

Yael turned toward him and scowled at the men closing in with guns at the ready.

She didn't lower hers. Instead, she asked, "The fuck are *you* doing here?"

Johnny huffed and tried to shut his robe over his belly, shaking his gun at her. "You come to my house and ask me -"

"Your house?" She made a face and nodded toward the mansion. "This isn't *your* house."

Tucking his weapon into the strap of his robe as he caught his breath, he scowled at her.

"No, but that is," he retorted hotly.

Looking past him, she eyed the house hidden beyond the security hut. It was nothing like the grande home to her right, but it was still large enough to stand tall over the lush landscaping. Shrugging, she started toward him and lowered her weapons.

When she passed him by, he threw his hands up and ran to cut her off, opening his arms to block her path.

"Why'd ya have to break Billy's nose, huh? Couldn't you have just made an appointment?"

Yael pointed her gun at *his* nose, a stony expression on her face. "Get the *fuck* out of my way, Johnny."

"Geez, kid. What's eatin' you?" he asked, ignoring the steel only inches away.

Her lip quivered and tears filled her eyes.

"Please, miss!"

To everyone's surprise, the youngest and newest member of the security detail dropped to his knees beside Yael. She tried to step away, but he fell forward and wrapped his arms around her legs to beg in a pitchy voice.

"They'll kill me for sure!"

Johhny made a face at him and saw Yael do the same as several of the guards groaned.

"Please!"

Yael rolled her eyes and stared at the sky. *"Dio Santo…"*

Johhny's chin shot up, shocked by her casual use of such a familiar phrase. "Parli Italiano?"

She met his eyes but didn't answer.

The Don's voice cracked over a walkie. *"You guys having a fucking party? And what the* fuck *is Luca doing on the ground?"*

"Begging, sir," a guard behind them answered, causing most of the others to snicker.

Though Luca hadn't moved at first, he was grinning sheepishly as he got to his feet. "At least it worked."

"Yeah, nice job," Johhny said sarcastically.

"Well? Mamma mia, *do I have to come down there myself?"*

Yael shook her head and threw the guard's weapon to the ground before holstering her own. "Tell him to make it quick."

Glowering at her defiance, Johhny waved everyone off and followed her up the walkway to the house.

"On the way, boss," Rocco grumbled, sending word to the Don via the walkie on his chest.

When Rocco fell in line behind them, head hanging in shame, Johhny hung back to give him a reassuring pat on the shoulder. Though he might have had more than a few words for his head of security tonight, Luca's display told him all he needed to know. Johhny was willing to bet that — per usual — Luca had abandoned his post at the side door out of boredom.

Moreover, Yael Phillips was technically a friend of the Family. An employee, really. Whatever happened tonight, the blame was on *her*.

The Don was already in his office, pacing as he concluded a conversation with a few choice words in Italian. He slammed the phone down and addressed Yael angrily, thumbing at his bulbous nose with a hard sniff.

"We have a way of doing things around here, young lady!"

"Get to the point, *Sammy*," she replied scathingly.

The Don's mouth dropped open.

"Alright, alright!" Johhny shouted, stepping between them.

Johhny looked at Yael and shook his head, face set firm to scold her silently. Ushering her into a seat, he turned to ask them both the same question.

"One o' you wanna explain what the hell's going on here?"

"Vitto's gone off the *fucking* rails!" the Don exploded.

Johhny paled. "Come again?"

He looked to Yael for answers, but her face went slack the moment she met his eyes. They both turned to face the Don.

He was pacing again. "They warned me, but no!"

Gloria's furry red kitten heels announced her presence before anyone could see her.

"Here!" she said as she burst into the room. The phone in her hand seemed to pull her to her husband. "Daddy was napping, but he's coming."

After she gave him the phone, she gawked at Yael and gasped. Closing her red see-through robe, she greeted Johhny, then turned her pointy nose up and tapped her way back out of the room.

Johhny stared at the ceiling and shook his head.

Rolling her eyes with a huff, Yael stood and faced the Don. "I'm out."

"Oh no you don't!" the Don blustered. "We need to talk about this."

But she was already walking out of the room. "No, *we* don't. I'm not waiting around all night. You've got twenty-four hours."

With that, she left.

Johhny watched as the Don stared at her back, then shrugged off her display. Seconds later he was greeting his elderly father-in-law with a soft tone of respect and honor. Johhny assumed they would deal with the girl later; removing a rogue enforcer trumped disciplining an insolent child throwing a tantrum. He wondered who was open right now because this situation *definitely* called for a meatball sub.

CHAPTER SIX

Telling herself she didn't want to wake Joe, Yael left South Tampa and drove back to Ybor. Tomorrow, she would tell him she hadn't been able to sleep and decided it best to go home – per their new arrangement. The truth was, she didn't want to have to explain the reason behind her sudden departure. Though she was sure he would probably be a little hurt, she would rather it be a little hurt than extremely upset.

She drove much slower as she crossed the city, thinking about how stupid and irresponsible she'd been earlier. She could have lost her life or hurt someone…or at the very least gone to jail. But as luck would have it, the city of Tampa was rather quiet on this humid Monday night.

Yael's first day in the light had been eventful to say the least. Her mind drifted back and forth between all the awful possibilities and the terrifying scene from her dream-turned-vision. When she reluctantly took the job as a hitman for the mafia, she could have tried a little harder to refuse.

If only she had known better.

If only she had found the light a little sooner.

What she hadn't been expecting was the response from her boss and handler tonight. *They* were supposed to have things under control. *They* were supposed to have the answers. Now, all she had was more questions.

As far as she knew, Vitto was just another hitman on the payroll. That was all she was able to gather from her previous calls with Johnny and the chaos tonight. He was also a mob cleaner — her cleaner. Obviously he wasn't cleaning…but why? Was the bloody mess he left a part of his twisted legacy or was he trying to get her caught? Was he doing this at every scene he was sent to clean — or just hers?

Being a vigilante the last few years meant she'd racked up *a lot* of bodies. Nothing ever tied her to the murders, as far as she knew. But what if she'd unknowingly left clues in her haste and fear to get away? What if the police found the scenes *he* left behind — but thought *she* was sicko?

Yael didn't know what was worse — being caught by a man like him or being caught by the police? And she hadn't thought of it until now, but she had to ask…

Was Vitto watching her?

Did he know who she was? Where she lived?

She sighed and decided right then he probably didn't know anything at all. He was just a psychopath? Or…was it sociopath?

Maybe I can find a book at the library on crazy killers?

You know…that's probably not the best idea.

She blanched and nodded in agreement.

Eleven minutes later, Yael pulled into the lot behind the manor and parked, feeling the sting of fearful tears breaking through her numbness. All she could hope was that her dream had come in time to warn her — but even that was a mystery.

After five years of dreaming in a blur, chasing her visions down for weeks on end with the hope of painting a clearer picture, now she was able to pull up the vision like a memory from a mental camcorder?

She shuddered. Why did it keep happening like this? If her dreams were some kind of *gift*, some sort of *power*…why did the 'upgrades' always come at such a horrifying price?

Her mind was so clouded that she walked up to the base of the trellis beneath her window out of habit. In all the years of climbing up and down, she couldn't recall a night where she was so tired. And to think, no one had to die tonight to bring about such deep exhaustion.

Shaking her head, she continued around to the front of the house and groaned. Sure, she was thankful she didn't have to climb two stories, but unfortunately the living room light was on. All she could do was hope Frederico had fallen asleep on the couch again.

Living with her cousin gave her a lot of freedom, but also a keeper she wasn't exactly thrilled to answer to. The last few months had been rough on their relationship and she couldn't handle lying to him right now.

Alright then, just fix your face.

Tears started to pool in her eyes the moment she tried.

"Shit."

If she couldn't lie to Frederico tonight, how did she expect to lie to Joe tomorrow? How was she going to do the one job assigned to her with the two most important men in her life watching her every move?

The snarl of a catfight in the darkness reminded her that she was still standing outside. Vulnerable to anyone. What would be worse — facing her cousin or an ambush by Vitto?

She shivered and quickly unlocked the door, ignoring her stomach turning about as she stepped inside to greet her cousin.

But he wasn't on the couch. The house was oddly silent.

"Cuz?"

His bedroom door was open but the light was off. She walked down the hallway and peered inside; his bed was empty.

"Fred?"

An eerie feeling crept over her, but she shook it off. His car *was* outside, but maybe he had someone pick him up?

Unable to make heads or tails of it all, she walked towards the stairs to go take a shower. If he wasn't home by the time she finished, she would give him a call.

To her surprise, the door at the top of the stairs was wide open. She knew she hadn't left it open. She would never. Swallowing nervously, adrenaline rushed into her system.

Why do I feel the urge to run?

Forcing herself up the steps, she pulled her gun from her waistband and tiptoed up halfway until she could see onto the second floor landing.

The attic steps were down.

Fuck me!

Her secret lair had been discovered — and certainly not by Fred. He'd always had an unreasonable fear of the space, so much that he refused to help her renovate it years ago, even with the promise of splitting it to give him a man cave. But if Fred wasn't downstairs, and he wasn't upstairs…

She moved faster, wondering why she hadn't come home first. Why did she go to the Don when Fred was the vulnerable one?

Her eyes adjusted to the darkness as she glanced into her room. She never left her door open. The lump in the middle of her bed confused her; she couldn't remember why she would have put the pillow there tonight, didn't even remember doing so. Continuing around the edge of the landing, she stepped onto the ladder and climbed up, keeping her head low.

When she reached the top, she pointed the gun into the attic as she searched for signs of Fred or Vitto. She was shocked to find that every drawer, cabinet, and box was open as far as she could see.

Shit...

Whoever was here had discovered her millions, uncovered her arsenal of guns, knives and weaponry. If they were still here, there was no doubt they would be armed.

Taking a step back to retreat, she tried to breathe and quiet the sound of thumping in her head. But just as she turned to descend the steps, she remembered the bloody mess Vitto made of the man in her vision.

No, Fred. Not you, too.

No, she would not let that be their end.

Gritting her teeth, she stepped to the side and over a small, overturned box of her mother's most delicate trinkets and finery.

Son of a -

A noise at the back of the attic caught her attention. She saw a flash of light and followed it, walking on the balls of her feet and deftly avoiding creaky floorboards.

By the time she made it to the opposite corner, her hands were shaking and sweaty. Spending her entire lifetime drowning in fear was not enough to prepare her for this moment. But still...

No one is killing me with my own damn weapon!

The light switch was hidden just on the other side of the column across from her. She peered around the corner and saw a large figure shining a flashlight on her knife collection. Bounding across the walkway, she crouched down to hide and take a breath.

One...

Two...

She jumped up, flipping on the switch as she took aim at the intruder.

"Cuz!"

Yael dropped the gun and gasped for air, panic overtaking her. She fell to her knees.

Frederico stared down at her in shock.

All he could ask was, "What the fuck?"

CHAPTER SEVEN

Thirty-six hours.

Thirty-six hours was all it took for Yael's life to change forever. She sat on the couch with a huff and flipped her phone shut. Responding to Joe's texts from this morning — and the others she'd ignored last night — was easier said than done.

"Celitha said she can pick him up again today, so we should be straight."

Yael glanced up at Frederico, distracted. "Okay…cool."

Fred plopped onto the couch next to her and gave her a look.

She caught his eye and frowned. "What?"

He smiled and rolled his eyes to the ceiling.

"What!"

Frederico shrugged. "Nothing, man."

Yael felt naked — exposed. Her cousin had managed to get *everything* out of her these last two days, and she didn't like the feeling one bit.

"So," she yawned with a languorous stretch, "what's next?"

Groaning, he stood and turned to look over the house. The living room floor was a mess, having become their trash pile for the day. Otherwise, Yael wasn't sure what else they had to do to complete the transformation.

"Let's deal with this first," he mumbled, thumbing towards the mound of cardboard, styrofoam, plastic bags, and random scraps they'd been avoiding for the last hour.

She stood and pocketed her phone. Hands on hips, she studied the heap before nodding in agreement.

"There's more in my trunk," she thought aloud.

Frederico sighed and pressed play on the boom box, then headed to the kitchen for trash bags.

For months, he had been worried about his son, Tres. Unable to contact his baby mother, there was nothing he could do to confirm his suspicions that something was wrong. Then, on Monday night only an hour after Yael left to pick up dinner and head over to Joe's, the police knocked on the door with a temporary custody form — and a kindergartner in tow.

To Fred's shock and dismay, his ex was now in dependency court. But it was clear he was also ecstatic and excited to say he was officially a full-time father. It was a job he took seriously.

The lump in Yael's bed the night she found Fred in the attic was no pillow, but rather, her six-year-old nephew. Frederico's lifelong fear of the attic disappeared the moment he realized all his childhood things were packed away; he wasn't going to wait for Yael to show up to find them. They both counted themselves lucky she didn't have an itchy trigger finger.

On Tuesday, Yael and Frederico worked to convert the trap house into a safe house, and not just for her nephew. Now that he knew about her nighttime activities and the new threat, Fred wasn't taking any chances. The locks had all been changed, and Yael's keys revoked. The only key she had left was to the newly installed lock on the door at the top of the stairs. Special kits to lock the windows in place were put in across the house, and the trellis outside Yael's window was cut in certain spots to make the climb impossible.

Frederico was coming to terms with Yael's double life, and his questions were becoming fewer as he began to truly understand who she was. Yes, she was a vigilante assassin. And yes, she received payments and accepted hits from the mafia — but that only started this year. He seemed to keep up with the yeses far better than the no's. The only thing Fred struggled to grasp was the one thing she couldn't explain: her dreams.

When he rescued her five years prior, he knew what she had done, why she had run. What he didn't know was how it all came to be. Yael found it easiest to start from the beginning, to explain the dreams that commenced after her mother died, to show him her journals as living proof of her curse.

It was obvious that he believed her. Notebooks or not, the stories she told him filled in all the gaps of their quiet existence over the years. He could see why she slept through the day, why her nightmares didn't stop after the immediate trauma passed. He could see how she saw the bars and nightclubs of Ybor City as a quiet sanctuary from the terrors of her own mind. He could see how she ended up trusting Xavier, the bastard. But what he could not see is how a normal Tampa girl could have premonitions and sixth senses about people she'd never met, didn't even know existed.

By the time they closed the last trash bag, the house looked how it always had. The sense of normalcy rang false in Yael's head, and she felt her stomach turn. Yes, the living room and dining room of Fred's red house were just as bare and dark as always.

But nothing was the same.

For the last five years, Yael slept in her mother's childhood bedroom and used her childhood furniture. When her parents got married her father whisked her mother away to Sicily, and then upon their return, settled in a new house across town. Her grandmother kept every single item in place — until her mother died.

When Yael came to live with Fred at just seventeen years old, she was delighted to find all her mother's high school things in the attic. Now, most of it was packed up and waiting for Yael to move it or store it.

Fred's second bedroom downstairs was now his son's room, and Yael's room upstairs housed all of Fred's storage and equipment. The attic was still Yael's lair, but all the guns, weapons, and gear would find a new home — once Yael found hers.

After years of wanting to move out — and being afraid he would try to stop her — she was being politely guided to get out as soon as possible. Yael understood. Her nephew was a handful, but he was an innocent who deserved the love and protection of the adults in his village.

And she wasn't the only one forced to build a new life.

Frederico sent word out across the neighborhood informing everyone that his son was home. After a massive blowout sale, he had managed to move all of the drugs out of the house in less than two days. No longer the hood dope man, he intended to focus on his technical craft instead. Yael was proud.

Frederico already had a strong relationship with Ybor business owners as the local IT guy, but his hood announcement also included information about his new offerings. Equipped with cameras and sound, he was set on becoming the connect for the growing number of rappers and musicians in the area. He'd even mentioned something about doing PR and press kits with his web design skills.

His porn site was becoming a cash cow and the sale of the

remaining drugs gave him a nice cushion, but he was not the type to sit around doing nothing. Next week, he would be renovating his office-turned-storage space across the lot into a sound studio. One thing was for certain, Fred was always ready for whatever came his way.

Yael...wasn't.

"Do you ever check on the victims?"

"Huh?"

Fred dropped the trash bags outside the front door. "I'm saying, you don't know what happened to the girls, right?"

Yael sighed. "I usually try to forget."

"Damn." Frederico shook his head. "That's real, though."

Yael nodded.

Her first official job with the mob had led her to a trailer one county over. The trailer had been equipped as a sex dungeon: chains, stocks, ball gags, the whole nine. The second man she killed that night was holding two underage Latina's hostage, drugging and abusing them for sport.

As she always did when she found an innocent that needed saving, she helped the girls escape. And, like always, she pushed the two young trafficking victims from her mind thereafter. Yael couldn't bear the thought of what the girls had faced, so pretending it never happened was the best way to move on.

Frederico was tough and had thick skin. But contrary to his reputation around the neighborhood, Yael knew him more as a fierce protector than a bully. Something in his eyes told her he wasn't going to give up as easily as she did — especially since he knew the men she'd taken out.

Every time Fred asked her about her life today, it was obvious her role in the Rizzoli deaths had gotten under his skin. Frederico never liked the three brothers, not many did; they were known to be violent and racist against anyone who wasn't Italian. Still, the Rizzoli brothers were his ex's cousins — Tres' only uncles. No one had seen or heard from the older brothers since the youngest was murdered atop a parking garage a few blocks away.

She couldn't blame Frederico for feeling the way he did — it was all too close to home. This was especially true, since Yael was the one to slit young Antoni's throat that night.

"I'm gonna try to find them, cuz."

Yael was startled. "Who?"

"The girls," he responded quietly. "Maybe if we can find them —"

"We?"

He crossed his arms. "Yeah, we. If *we* can find them, maybe we can find out who the Rizzoli's were working with?"

She took a deep breath, trying to stay calm. Swallowing nervously, she asked, "Then what?"

Fred opened his mouth to speak, then snapped it shut. "I'on even know, cuz."

Yael didn't answer, couldn't really.

Johhny and the Don called her last night with an update, but there wasn't much to tell. After all, Vitto came from a long line of mafia enforcers and cleaners, and the best cleaners lived off the grid. Even if they had a wife, kids, a whole family — nobody would ever know.

She knew Johhny and the Don would likely be occupied with Vitto for a while. But it probably wouldn't hurt to ask what they knew about the uptick in human trafficking around the Port, right?

Yael bit her lip, then let out a sharp exhale. "Okay."

"Okay?" Frederico perked up.

"Let's do it. Let's find them."

"WHAT DO YOU THINK?"

Frederico looked around the room and smiled. "He gon' love it, cuz."

Yael smiled back, genuinely pleased by their efforts today.

Fred's longtime junk room was now a proper bedroom for his son, with tiny furnishings and toys from IKEA set up around a giant play carpet in the center of the room. She felt like a proud parent awaiting their newborn, but this was no nursery and the circumstances were nowhere near as sweet.

For six long years, Frederico's ex had stuck to her promise.

Serafina Rizzoli told him plainly: she would ruin his life if he left her. The second-to-last time he tried to break up with her was just after Yael moved in. Fred was used to Serafina's abuse and threats, so he didn't take her seriously. A few months later, a drunken night of mistakes led to a baby being conceived. When he denied her again, she lost her mind and had been trying to destroy his life through his own son.

Frederico couldn't help but be aware of her hatred — and that his son was beginning to embody it all too well — but he had no idea she was also abusing and neglecting the only pawn she had in this game. Now she'd lost her meal ticket (and the child support that went along with it), leaving Fred his first real chance at fatherhood.

Smiling as her cousin stepped into the room to reorder the cars in the HotWheels case, Yael couldn't help but feel overwhelmed knowing what he might face. He didn't look much like a father; in fact, he looked exactly the same as he had in high school. His signature outfit of basketball shorts and a crisp black tee kept him young. But there was something in his eyes the last few days, something undeniably mature. Tall and handsome as ever, something about the way he moved said he was finally becoming the man he always wanted to be.

Yael left the doorway and stepped into the bathroom to wipe her eyes. Her phone buzzed.

Shit.

Joe was texting her again, this time sending a single question mark. She had no idea what to say, and she knew it was killing them both. The last time she disappeared, Joe was devastated. Wasn't it only couple weeks ago that she made him a promise not to do this again? Yet here she was.

Frederico called to her as he stepped into the hall. "Where you stayin' tonight?"

Yael pocketed her phone with a grimace. "Westin again."

"Your boyfriend don't want you at the house?"

Sticking her tongue out and making a face, she walked into the kitchen to pour a glass of water. Fred didn't need to know *everything*.

"He's not my boyfriend," she corrected. "And I told you already, we're taking things slow."

"How slow?"

She eyed him over the top of her glass.

He smirked. "I'm saying, why don't you tell him the truth?"

Yael nearly choked. "About what?"

"Everything?" Frederico grinned when he saw her face turn pale. "Okay, some things? At least the fact that you homeless now."

She frowned. He blushed.

"My bad cuz, you ain't homeless -"

"It's fine, Fred."

They both took a beat to breathe. Being roommates for five

years and cousins for life made the transition feel like an ending. Yael didn't like endings.

Frederico tried to recover. "Just play it cool, cuz. Remember, you're not technically a criminal…unless you get caught."

Rolling her eyes, Yael said a silent prayer. Not that she couldn't trust her cousin — she just didn't want to kill him. Clearing her throat, she turned to ask him the million dollar question.

"So how do you want to do this?"

Eyes darting side to side, he asked, "Do what?"

She shrugged. "I don't know…fight the traffickers, I guess?"

Fred crossed his arms and chewed at his lip. "You can leave me those notebooks? Or you need them?"

"I don't know…"

Yael's vision from Monday night was still clear as day, and there were no other kills on the docket. Her journals were cryptic and confusing, even for her; but if Fred could help her figure things out, it couldn't hurt.

Frederico placed a hand on her shoulder. "I wish you could stay, cuz."

"Me too," she said plainly, the numbness setting in again. "I'll bring you the rest of the notebooks once I get settled, but you can keep the ones upstairs for now. I'll have to explain my system, though. Otherwise they'll be no use to you."

"Aight."

She paused and stared at him. "Please don't let anyone see them."

"Ain't nobody finna be in this house but me, cuzzo."

Yael smirked. "And your lady friends."

"Hell nah. I'm done with women, seeing what women did to my jit."

"I'm a woman."

Frederico let out a loud harrumph as he dropped onto the couch. "I guess."

"Whatever," she tossed back. "Just promise me you'll be careful. The Don said there's a shit storm brewing with this Vitto situation and I don't want you caught up in that. I don't think any of this is connected, but now that you got baby boy we can't exactly risk things."

"That's real."

She sighed. "Alright, cuz. I'mma head out."

Yael heard kissing sounds coming from the living room. When she turned, Fred was standing with his back to her, rubbing his arms up and down.

"Shut up, Fred!"

CHAPTER EIGHT

The next day, Yael found herself anxiously watching the clock. It had been three days since she spoke with Joe, and tonight she planned on showing up at his place with the hopes of explaining her latest conundrum. She'd been thinking about him a lot, which made for a clumsy shift.

But soon she would be free. And that was very good news, because tonight was Throwback Thursday, Margarita's most popular karaoke night. The all-you-can-eat fajita special brought the people in, but it only took a couple drinks for patrons to realize what a *perfect* time it was to sing their favorite song from high school. The regulars even used it as a chance to dress up in their vintage gear, turning back the clock on stage for an inebriated crowd.

Margarita's was one of the largest restaurants on the strip and the only one with a full patio and outdoor bar. Even with the karaoke machine and stage set up outside on the patio, there was no escaping the sound. The large French doors connecting the two spaces were only closed on club nights. No one had performed a song yet, but the crowd outside was getting louder and drunker thanks to the encouragement of the DJ.

Won't be long now...

Eileen and Jeanne, two of her regulars, had spent the last hour complaining about the noise. The epitome of the idiom 'opposites attract', Eileen was tall, black, and bourgeois and Jeanne was a short, self-proclaimed "Florida Cracker". If you didn't know they were friends, you would assume they were mortal enemies — other patrons often did.

When Yael started working for Ricardo as a dishwasher four years ago, she was looking for a distraction. It wasn't until she started tending the bar that Eileen and Jeanne showed up, and she had to admit she was grateful for their incessant chatter — most of the time. But some days — like today — she found them to be the most annoying women on earth.

For as long as she could remember, the pair would post up at the end of her bar and people-watch. Having nothing better to do, they would give pedestrians silly voices and cook up crazy reasons for those rushing down the strip. This afternoon's rambunctious crowd gave them all the ammo they needed. Their little game often reminded her of her mother, who did the same thing whenever they were waiting in line or walking through the mall when she was young.

Yael imagined that Eileen's wardrobe was packed with colorful pantsuits, because she'd never seen the woman wear anything else. The dated outfits, jewelry, and accessories were always put together in such a way that Eileen appeared to have walked off the cover of a Jet Magazine from the 1980s. Jeanne's outfits were also out of the 80s, though she preferred bedazzled jean jackets and t-shirts signed by rockers of the past. The only thing they seemed to have in common was a pair of matching beer bellies.

Yael glanced up at the clock behind her. *Ten more minutes.* Sure each one would drag on with the two chatty Kathy's present, she busied herself with refilling the condiment holders.

"Now who does she think she is?"

Jeanne shook her head. "Can you believe that?"

"I'm not saying a word, honey. Hmph!"

Yael peered over the bar and saw a shapely woman standing just outside the doorway. Her white tube top and short skirt were skimpy and see through, revealing the outline of tattoos on her hips and bottom. Her hair was in a high ponytail and she appeared to be enjoying herself.

Rolling her eyes at women across from her, Yael put the jars away and headed outside to stock the other bar. Just as she reached the doorway to the patio, the woman in white abruptly turned and ran right into her. She was obviously well into her cups and struggling to find her balance. She placed a hand on Yael's forearm to steady herself.

"Where's the bathr -"

Yael froze.

The woman looked her up and down critically. "You!"

Yael stared into the eyes of the woman she hoped to never see again. The woman who represented everything she wanted to forget. The woman who served as a living reminder of a dead man's tale…Yael felt as if she'd seen a ghost.

"Stacey?" she whispered.

Stacey's eyes lit up. "Bitch! Where is he?"

Gasping when the drunken finger poked her square in the chest, Yael tried to back away.

But Stacey took a step forward. "Tell me! I know you know!"

Yael couldn't speak, couldn't move. The walls seemed to close in on her, and she suddenly felt very warm. This wasn't supposed to be happening. Xavier was dead!

"Bitch, are you fuckin' listenin' to me?"

Stacey was screaming and slurring, her pale skin flushed, her beautiful features contorted into an ugly rage face.

Eileen's deep, eloquent voice cut through the tension as she came to loom over them. "Excuse me?"

"What's the problem here, eh?" Jeanne asked, hands perched on her wide hips.

Yael swallowed, eyes darting between the two women standing on either side of her aggressor. Stacey didn't seem to care.

"You stupid -"

"No!" Jeanne interrupted, bumping Stacey with her belly. "You don't talk to *her*, you talk to *me*."

"Or you can talk to me," Eileen countered, bouncing a stumbling Stacey off her belly as well.

Jeanne snapped her fingers in front of Stacey's face. "But you *don't* talk to *her*."

"Yaya?"

Looking to the door, Yael almost fainted when the night's bouncers, Dallas and Bear, walked in for their shifts. Tilting her head down at Stacey, she backed away in retreat.

Stacey let out a growl of frustration. "Fuck you, bitch!"

Her back was to the scene, but Yael could see them in the mirror ahead. Stacey's legs kicked through the air as the bouncers carried her out, screaming all the way.

"I'll be back, bitch. I got you now!"

Eileen smiled and waved her fingers. "We'll be waiting!"

"Yeah, toodles!" Jeanne quipped.

Embarrassed, Yael went to squat behind the bar until the end of her shift.

"You alright?"

Looking up for the source of the melodic sound, she met Eileen's smiling eyes. The tall woman was gazing down at her cheerfully, her chin resting on her hands with her elbows on the bar.

Yael stood and cleared her throat, surprised to find Jeanne next to Eileen in the same position. Clearing her throat again, she smirked at the odd couple before her.

"Of course. Next round's on me."

"You don't gotta pay us, kiddo."

Eileen nodded in agreement. "Yeah, we're your best friends!"

Staring blankly at the women, she found it hard to disagree — hard as she might try. Not that they knew anything about her...but no one else did, either. Ybor City was like a small town where everybody knows your name. Now that she wasn't destined to a life in the darkness, it was time to make better use of the light.

I need to get out more.

Handing them both a drink, she gave them a small smile.

"Drink up, drunkies."

CHAPTER NINE

Yael was numb, staring coldly into dead eyes. The man she had just killed was the least of her worries. A *knowing* within her said there was no time to waste. Soon, she would be on the outside looking in, watching *him*.

She shuddered, knowing he might be close by. And what if…he was closer than she thought?

It was time to leave, but something felt off. Turning about the small living room, she searched her mind's eye, trying to remember what her vision said would come next. She knew she was having doubts about the mental download she'd received Monday night, even though she could still see it clearly a few days later.

Pushing the vision from her mind all week was no easy feat, but it didn't matter. Her knowledge of this kill came from a memory implanted before she lived it. Relying on her old notes system was rudimentary, but at least the process gave her the chance to ease into the *where* and *how* of murdering her next victim. When it came down to living out the dream, she would find peace in following the *knowing* — the undeniable feeling of déjà vu — because in many ways it felt like she was a part of the plan. This new clarity

51

went beyond foresight; it was a stark reminder of the powerlessness of her position.

In the final moments of her vision, she would need to look through a window. There was only one window in this room. It dawned on her that she wouldn't be able to see *him* through the curtains if they were closed.

At least he wasn't watching me first.

She kicked a stack of newspapers, sliding them towards the space under the windowsill until they held the edge of the curtain in place. When she turned to face the body, she found it was almost the same vantage point she had in her vision.

Of course, she had no interest in seeing this scene up close and personal. And being within a stone's throw of such a disgusting man was the last thing she wanted. But tonight wasn't about *him*. It was about her — and this curse.

Tonight would be her proof, that she was in fact able to see the future. If the vision played out any different, she'd be sure it was a fluke. But the only way to be sure was for her to play her part. She had to show up. She had to look through the window.

Show up and look through the window.

That's it.

At least that was the speech she'd been replaying in her head all day. She tried being encouraging; she tried being fierce; she even tried reverse psychology.

Somehow, she wasn't afraid to commit murder — but she was to afraid to look through a window? Really? Such cowardice!

The truth was, Yael couldn't see what happened *after* she looked through the window. And there wasn't a single cell in her body that wanted to find out.

She turned off the lights and stepped into the darkness from the side door. Closing it silently and dialing Johhny in the process, she searched her surroundings. He answered on the third ring.

"It's done," she barked.

"Well, hello to you, too."

"Whatever, Johhny." The crack in her voice was telling.

"You alright there?"

"Yeah, I'm fine," she lied, trying to steady herself.

Johhny paused for a beat. "You know we have other guys…"

"You wanna tip him off? Besides, you said it yourself: this is a high value kill, I'm the best you've ever had."

Johhny let out an ugly snort.

"And, we agreed to keep it business as usual, remember?"

"Yeah, I remember."

Yael looked at the receiver, noting the distance in his reply. Shaking it off, she cut the conversation short. "I'll be at the bar this weekend. See you around."

Flipping her phone shut and shoving it into her back pocket, Yael turned the corner behind a neighbor's fence and walked to the next street where her car was parked. It was late and the neighborhood was relatively quiet for a Friday night. Sticking to the shadows, she made her way around and hopped into her car. She drove down the block, stopped at the stop sign, and waited.

Yael couldn't remember how long she was supposed to sit here, but she didn't have time to think about it. A car started at the opposite end of the street and crept along the road with its lights off. She wasn't able to make out anything other than it being a dark sedan; it stopped at the stop sign on the other end of the street…and waited.

It hadn't occurred to her that Vitto could be so close. She assumed he would await Johhny's call for the cleanup request, but she was also assuming that Vitto was unaware they were onto him.

Being in the same city, the same zip code as this monster was unnerving. But for some reason, the idea that he might already be in the neighborhood was a thought she previously categorized as paranoid and irrational.

Maybe not?

Turning the wheel, she sped off into the night, wondering if she could catch the car before it made a move. Turning onto the next street, she tapped on her brights and raced down the block.

But it was gone.

Shit.

Yael put the car into park and tried to steady her fast beating heart. It had only been a couple minutes since she left the house. So, the best way to determine if Vitto was already on her tail was to check the house now. But that meant she would risk running into him. And even if she was able to escape his grasp, he'd know she knew.

And where would that put me?

A car approaching from the main road set off her alarm bells. Luckily, she could see the small, elderly woman inside the silver Civic when she passed.

Unless…

She laughed and shook herself, not sure which thought had been funnier: that the little lady was his driver and he was hiding in the trunk — or that Vitto's big secret was that he was actually a tiny woman.

If only.

A chill went down her spine.

Show up and look through the window. That's it.

"That's it."

Yael made the first right turn, and then the second. Doing her best to keep her speed slow enough to check things out and fast enough that she wouldn't draw attention, she did something she had never done before: return to the scene of a crime.

A few new cars were parked along the street, but she hadn't been paying enough attention to be sure of anything else. She did know where she would park this time around to ensure a fast and easy getaway, so she made her way to the empty house and parked alongside an old RV.

Two minutes later, she was staring at the ray of light shining from the window she sought. Denial set in, but she couldn't pretend. She hadn't left any lights on.

Fucking fuck.

And so it was. She was here. She showed up. Now, it was time...

Though she wished it was because she was being careful, Yael knew the real reason why she moved so slowly. This wasn't the first time her legs had turned to jelly and she was certain it wouldn't be the last.

The ledge outside the window gave her just enough to grip as she squatted to look through the small triangular opening she'd left herself. She found the chair the man was sitting on when she killed him, but the body was gone. Trying her left eye and a new angle, she followed movement and realized both men were on the floor in front of the couch.

Oh, God.

The man was tall and gangly, with slick black hair. He wore a long black shirt and had his dark, thick-rimmed glasses resting on his forehead. The long, spindly fingers of one hand were wrapped around the hilt of a long blade; the other hand held a large mason jar.

Yael frowned.

Though she had all week to come to terms with what would

happen here tonight, she was having trouble processing what she was seeing.

How long had it been since she called Johhny?

Carefully sliding her phone out of her back pocket, she checked the call time and lost her breath. Unless he brought extra blood with him, Vitto had somehow filled a large mason jar almost halfway in just over ten minutes. Unfortunately, Yael didn't know enough about this kind of thing to know what this meant. She'd seen men bleed out quickly…maybe half a jar wasn't much at all?

The bile rising in her throat brought one question to her mind.

Now what?

Everything in her said she should kill him where he stood. She couldn't help but agree. But just as she pulled out her gun, she saw a flash of red.

Vitto was painting the pale yellow walls with the deep red blood, stopping every few splashes to admire his work.

Stomach roiling, Yael gagged as she tried to stop herself from vomiting. Just as she successfully choked it down, she let out an involuntary cough.

Vitto stopped mid splash and turned to look at the side door. Yael watched his back lift slowly on an inhale and marveled at his calm. But when he turned on his heel and stared into her left eye, she fell backwards into the dirt, immobilized by fear.

He screamed, a primal, guttural noise Yael hoped never to hear again. It was enough, all she needed to spring into action. In seconds, she was running through the neighborhood back the way she came, blinded by terror and thick, salty tears.

CHAPTER TEN

Yael rode down Joe's street for the fourth time that week. He hadn't text her in days, and hadn't called either. If he wasn't home this time, she was going to have to suck it up and call him. As much as she'd like to apologize and explain in person, she knew she'd already gone too far.

She pulled up at the corner of Shell Point and Mistic Point, stopping at the edge of four separate driveways where all the properties met on the street. The large homes to her right were secured by motorized gates; Joe's house was straight ahead via the only unpaved driveway. The first time she'd come here, she wouldn't have imagined the most beautiful house on the block would be down that dirt road beyond the overgrown bushes and trees.

Joe's property was massive, and like all the houses on this street, the backyard overlooked the Bay. The front lawn ran the length of the driveway, which led to a paved incline in front of the three-car garage. Lush landscaping stretched all the way down both sides of the property. Thick bushes and flowering trees had been planted along the red brick steps leading to the wraparound porch.

The big, blue majestic cottage was nestled between four mature pecan trees; from the edge of the drive the mansion appeared smaller than it actually was.

Where the front of the property was shady and dim, the back of the house was bright, open, and airy. A teakwood boardwalk connected the driveway to the long dock at the edge of the backyard. Sand colored pavers and white furniture brought a resort feel to the space, with the tall palm trees and saw palmettos replacing the more traditional landscaping of the front yard. Joe's favorite place was his garden on the side of the house; Yael often caught him outside watering the seedlings and fawning over the more mature plants.

Inside, the design style was what Yael thought of as muted masculine. The first story included the dining room, living room, den, and a study. She had only been inside Joe's bedroom upstairs, but she was sure there were at least seven doors in the hallway. The interior design favored the front of the house, with rich colors like tan, pewter, and navy on the walls and furniture.

When she disappeared on him the first time, Joe did a lot of work on the landscaping and finished the last touches of the home renovation he'd taken on. Though it had been less than a week since she ran off, she had a sinking feeling that things would again be different. The bushes didn't seem so unkempt and the grass that lined the street had been trimmed.

She pulled up to examine the street, wondering if the city had come to take care of the whole road. To her surprise, Joe's car was parallel parked on the grass, as was a sleek, silver Mercedes AMG. Yael didn't know what to think.

As usual, her timing couldn't be worse. Joe was suddenly there, walking down the dirt path that was his driveway with a pretty lady.

Arm in arm, they laughed merrily and made their way onto the street.

Yael was stunned. It had only been a few days and he'd already moved on? Or maybe he'd been seeing this woman when she came back last month? Whatever the case, she wanted to disappear before —

Joe met her eyes, but his face said nothing. He continued his banter with the lady in the nice suit, his tone more subdued though still friendly. He hugged her back when she threw her arms around his neck, and gave her his cheek to kiss. Opening her car door, he smiled and gave her a wave as she drove down the street with a double tap of her horn.

Devastation came in waves, and Yael thought seriously about driving off to save him the trouble of explaining. His face gave her no indication that he wanted to see her, and he didn't seem at all worried that she'd caught him with the woman.

Who is she?

Whoever she was, Yael was sure she was a girl Joe could take home to his parents. Simple. What more could he desire?

She met his eyes, swallowing when she saw his look of expectation.

No, she couldn't drive off. Joe was not the type of man to leave things open.

Sighing, Yael pulled forward and parked behind him. When he didn't come to open her door, the tears began to flow. Wiping her eyes furiously, she opened the door and walked to the driveway to meet him.

Handsome as ever in a tailored blue suit, Joe's long dreadlocks were piled upon his head as he often did after a long day. Yael's tears increased when she thought of the woman running her fingers through his hair, helping him get comfortable...

"Where have you been?"

Though she could not understand why, the question was like a dagger to her heart. She promised him she wouldn't disappear again, but she did exactly that. How could she explain?

Standing before him, she lost her nerve. One knee gave way beneath her, the wobble spreading through her whole body as she struggled to find the words to make him understand.

When Joe crushed her to him, it was none too soon. She melted into his arms and heard the small sob escape her before she could stop it.

Whether it was three seconds or three minutes, she couldn't tell. All she knew was things still hadn't changed between them. Every hug they shared felt like a release. And after the week she'd had, this embrace was the sweetest thing she'd ever known.

Yael lifted her nose to smell his cologne; she'd missed him more than she realized. Unable to hold back, she kissed his neck softly and nuzzled against him.

Joe jumped away, placing his hands firmly on her shoulders with a grunt. Then he turned on his heel and marched to the house.

Barely able to walk as the devastation returned, she followed him inside, wondering how she would get him back this time.

YAEL SAT STIFFLY at the end of the couch, an awful sense of déjà vu creeping over her.

The last time she disappeared, she was gone for over two months. Still — whether five days or five months — it was obvious Joe didn't see a difference. Though it would pain her to do so, she had to at least try to fix this.

"I'm sorry, Joe."

"What?"

Frowning, she met his eyes. *Nothing.* "I said 'I'm sorry'."

"What for?"

Her frown deepened. Was he testing her or did he simply not care anymore? "I'm sorry for - for -"

"Ahh, you're not sorry."

"Hey! That's not fair!"

"No," Joe said angrily, looking down his nose at her. "You know what isn't fair? I don't even know your name, woman!"

"Yes, you do!"

He shook his head. "How am I supposed to know if you're dead or just run off again?"

"I didn't run off, Joe."

Joe threw his hands up. "You disappeared in the middle of the night!"

"I'm a grown woman, Joe! I have things to do, you know?"

"Oh, okay."

Yael frowned. This was *not* how this was supposed to be going. "I'm trying to apologize and you aren't making it easy."

"What makes you think I trust anything you say?"

Gasping softly, Yael dropped her head. He wasn't wrong. Deep down, she knew that. She hated that it still hurt to hear.

"Jessum peace, Yaya. You driving me mad, woman."

Joe crossed the living room and knelt in front of her. Yael couldn't look at him. She didn't know what to say.

"Last time you wouldn't even tell me where you gone. And you promised me you wouldn't run off again...can you really blame me?"

She shook her head. Tears fell down her face, but she didn't try to wipe them away. The numbness had set in.

"Yaya," Joe started again, nudging her chin up. "What happened?"

Looking into his eyes, she found the glimmer of hope she needed. "I'm homeless."

"Say what?"

Yael giggled. "I mean, not *homeless* homeless, but…wait, let me backtrack."

Joe scooped her into his arms and carried her to the other side of the couch, pulling the lever so they could recline. Wiping the tears from her face, he took her hand and kissed it.

"Continue."

"Well, technically I guess I *am* homeless. But that's not really the issue."

Yael proceeded to explain all that happened to lead to her house hunting, including a few extra details about Frederico and his ex to help Joe see the bigger picture. When he asked her why she needed to move out, she had to think on her feet. She told him that her cousin would look better to the court if he could prove he was capable of caring for his son without assistance, and Joe agreed.

"You hear these kinds of stories about baby mommas, but I never knew anyone who dealt with dependency court."

Yael nodded in agreement. "I always hear guys talk about child support, but I've never seen anyone get custody like this."

"Have you talked to the mother?"

She made a face. "That girl is crazy."

Joe chuckled. "Your cousin probably told you that."

"Nope. She's seriously off. They were broken up when I first moved in, but they still messed around. One night she threatened to kill herself if he made her leave."

Joe was shocked. "Wow."

"I know…If I hadn't of been there, Fred would probably be in jail or worse. The girl grabbed a butcher knife from the kitchen and ran into his bathroom. After about an hour, I told her he left and that I called the police to "Baker Act" her. She climbed out the window! I haven't spoken to her since."

A look of concern crossed his features. "Where was the boy then?"

Yael groaned. "*That* was the night he was conceived."

Joe closed his eyes and shook his head. "Terrible. I'm sorry you've had to deal with all that."

"*I'm sorry*, Joe. I came by almost every night this week to try to explain in person, but -"

"I wasn't home," he interrupted with a sigh.

"You weren't home."

Pulling her to him, he wrapped her up in his arms and nuzzled his face into her neck.

"I was working," he whispered huskily. "Why didn't you just call me, hmm?"

Goosebumps spread across her body as she sighed into his embrace.

"Next time, use your phone," he breathed into her lips.

He nibbled at her bottom lip, then kissed her, sparking a flash of electricity. The surge between them was not as much of a shock as the first time, but the burst of light hadn't happened since then either. She blinked.

"Yael...Phillips."

Joe stopped kissing her, but kept his lips against hers. "What?"

"That's my name," she whispered. "Yael Phillips."

"Yael," he kissed her softly, "Phillips."

"Mhm."

"Yael...I like this."

She giggled, enjoying the sound of her name on his tongue.

"Now you."

"Me, what?"

"Tell me something. How was work?"

Joe groaned. "Stressful."

"We can talk about it," she offered sweetly, hoping to finally return the favor of a listening ear.

"Actually, we can't."

Yael bit her lip. "Oh."

"No, no. No fret up yuself. I mean, I really can't talk about my work."

"Oh?"

"I can tell you where I was this week. I just interviewed for a special project; if I get it, I promise I'll tell you what I can."

"So…what do you do? Are you…a spy?"

Joe chuckled. "Not so glamorous. I'm just an agent."

Yael froze.

"Don't worry! It's mostly paperwork."

She saw the slight lift of his brow and gasped. "You're lying to me!"

Grinning, Joe hid his face. "Okay, maybe some interviews."

Yael shook her head, mouth open in disbelief. "I can't believe you."

"Alright, *Yael*," he said, adding emphasis to her name. "You got me. I am an FBI agent, and my job is very dangerous. I investigate killers of the worst kind."

Heart sinking into her stomach, Yael tried not to react.

"Hey," he said softly, "don't worry about me. I'm only teasing."

She did her best to breathe, but she was having trouble processing the meaning of all she just learned. The first man she truly ever loved wasn't supposed to be her enemy…but it seemed he would be by default.

"I have an idea."

Yael shook herself and met his eyes.

"Come," he said softly, sliding her legs off his lap. "Maybe we can help each other."

Following him warily, she put on her shoes and walked out the front door.

"I've been trying to sell the property for a few months, but the market isn't on my side. Sandra just staged the bungalow for me today, would you like to see it?"

Yael couldn't decline, though she had no earthly idea what he was talking about. So she nodded and followed him across the garden towards the house next door.

"Wait, where are we going?"

Joe looked at her quizzically and pointed up at the long white house ahead of them.

"That's yours, too?"

Laughing, he nodded and helped her step over a small mound of soil.

She had never paid the little building much attention, especially since she usually arrived for her visits in the evening. The first time she had come here, the area alongside the bungalow was blocked by landscaping supplies and construction equipment. As of late, the ivy that spread down the stark white wall was thick enough to blend into the surrounding tree line. But mostly, she and Joe never spoke of anything important, including his real estate ventures.

When they arrived at the front door, Yael fell in love.

The house was long, but not very wide. The trees blocking the front entrance had been cut back the day before to better frame the beautiful full-width porch. Tire marks in the dirt revealed a narrow one-way path to the rear of the property. Something about it said 'home' to Yael and from the very moment she saw it, she hoped she could stay.

Joe had painted the entire house white, leaving only the various light woods in their original stain. When they walked in, she was surprised to find everything inside was just as stark white: the marble flooring, the textured wallpaper, and the eat-in kitchen were all different bright and airy shades of white. The white furniture was modern; the paintings on the wall were reminiscent of Clearwater Beach. The open floor plan went straight through to the back of the house, starting with the living room and ending with a long wall of cabinets behind the kitchen.

"This used to be all one floor and everything was closed in, but I wanted to build up and give it more function. There's a garage now where the single bedroom used to be, and upstairs you have the bathroom, a huge closet, and the loft bedroom. What do you think?"

Yael was in awe.

Financially, there was no doubt she could afford it. Still, she couldn't help but wonder if it was wise for her to move in next door. That wasn't exactly *taking things slow...*

But when she followed him up to the second floor, she was sold. At the top of the stairs, the second level seemed to open up to the world outside. She realized the back wall of this floor was made entirely of thick glass. Her view of the bay was unreal.

"Out here is the roof of the garage. As you can see, both walls extend out. You can sit up here and watch the sunrise...or out there and sunbathe in privacy. There's a patio set along the wall, but you can't see it from here. The steps are in the garage and the door flips up...I'll show you later.

"The best part of all this is the view. If you walk out of the garage and down the path, you have a small but very private beach all to yourself. The mangroves are thick on either side, separating your beach and my dock, so you won't have to worry about me spying on you."

"Joe, it's like a painting! This is heaven."

"That was the goal. Blue skies above, blue water below...up here, you're in the clouds."

"Mhm."

Joe showed her the fully furnished bedroom, the bathroom with a Roman shower and deep soaking tub, and a closet she didn't think she would ever be able to fill.

His excitement about the secret balcony above the porch made her giddy. They sat on the small swing and watched the sun set beyond the trees through the slats of the roof.

"Are you sure you want me this close?"

"Closer," he said, squeezing her tight.

"I'm serious, Joe. This place is beautiful, but..."

"But?"

"I don't want to mess this up."

Joe made a sound, but didn't say a word.

She gave him a nudge. "Real nice."

"When I built this house, I wanted it to feel like a small piece of paradise away from everything. There are only a few places on the property where we would be able to see each other. Otherwise, you would have your privacy and I would have mine."

She nodded, realizing she had already forgotten they were just next door.

"Yael Phillips, I want to be with you."

Looking into his eyes, she knew all he spoke was truth. "I want to be with you, Joe."

"Then come and stay here. Be with me here. Say yes."

Yael kissed him soundly. "Yes."

SEPTEMBER

CHAPTER ELEVEN

Yael was running late, but that was nothing new. After years of living life in the darkness, she had grown accustomed to getting to her destinations quickly in the dead of night. The traffic and clutter of everyday life would take some getting used to.

She wasn't exactly in the best mood, either. When she got the call last week that she was being summoned for the reading of a will, she felt like her whole world came crashing down. Try as she might to rebuild, she had a feeling the funk wouldn't leave her system until the meeting occurred. One would think she would move quickly and do all she could to be on time today, but here she was nearly twenty minutes behind schedule.

Luckily, she had been at work only a few blocks away from the attorney's office. She knew she could still make it to the meeting on time if she skipped changing her clothes, so she opted to head straight there instead. She was a little nervous, meeting him face to face for the first time. But then again, he didn't seem to hold her in very high regard. Maybe it was best to keep it that way; playing stupid and lowly was becoming one of her specialities.

Staring up at the building with a twinge of loathing, she

wondered if she was in the right place. Having passed the office many a time, she felt ill. For months, she'd been completely unaware that the man who held the answers to Xavier's disappearance was in walking distance. If Yael's assumptions were correct, each time her ex had told her he was traveling the world, he was actually *incarcerated*. She believed the only way to contact Xavier was through this man, his attorney. The old wooden door read *Randolph & Associates*, letting her know she was in the right place.

When she finally made it inside, she was dripping with sweat. Pulling her fan from her pocket and realizing she was still wearing her bar apron, she looked at herself in the glass and tried to at least fix her hair.

Geez. Lowly indeed.

A low, droll voice caught her attention.

"We really don't need to wait any longer, do we?"

"Yes, sir. Unfortunately, we do."

"Pity. I wasn't aware there was anyone out there who cared so much about my family legacy."

"Believe me, there isn't."

Both men turned at the sound of her voice, but the young Brit slouching in the leather chair rose when his eyes landed on her face. At just over six feet, he was impeccably dressed in a grey suit and smelled like a rich, lush forest.

"And who might you be?" he asked with a bow and flourish.

Yael made a face. "Let's just get started."

"No?" he said, excitement spreading across his features. "We were waiting for *her*?"

"Yes, sir," the attorney replied curtly.

"This is wonderful! Madame, there is no need to divide the estate. I would be happy to marry you."

"Excuse me?" Yael choked out, looking at the attorney with wide eyes.

The older man clasped his hands together calmly. "My apologies, miss."

Turning toward the man invading her personal space, she asked, "Who are you?"

"Your betrothed of course, but you may call me Olivier."

"Olivier?"

"Dear me, like music to my ears."

"I'm already betrothed, and even if I wasn't, I came here today to sever ties not bind new ones. Now, let's get on with this — I've got work to do."

For a beat, Olivier stood frozen in shock by her dismissal. Recovering quickly, he ran to pull her chair back. Yael gave him a look, but he sat beside her unabashed and smiled at the attorney.

"Yes, let's begin," the attorney replied, obviously flustered. "Ms. Piccirrilo, my name is Sampson Whitney Randolph. It is a pleasure to finally meet you."

She gave him a curt nod, doing her best to hold her head high.

"Philomena Piccirrilo," he said to Olivier, extending his palm her way.

Yael shuddered at the use of her real name, but said nothing.

"The gentleman is Mr. Hill's first cousin. May I present to you Lord Olivier Maxwell Hulley, the third, 15th Earl of Ravenscar."

"Hi."

"Hi," Olivier replied huskily.

Sampson blinked. "We are here today to discuss the dissolution of the trust first established in 1988. Ms. Piccirrilo has requested a transfer. As the last living beneficiary of Mrs. Hill's trust, she will have the final say in how we proceed. If you will turn your attention to the screen, I have the breakdown here..."

Yael tried her best to listen intently, but much of what was said went over her head. The attorney did confirm that she was now the sole owner of most of Xavier's assets, all of his accounts, and had a legal claim to a vast majority of his inheritance.

Olivier finally spoke up.

"They were never married, so how is this possible?"

"Though they never went through with the marriage, the assets were transferred in a separate contract between the betrothed. Now, there are certain stipulations for the inheritance that did require a ceremony, such as the transfer of title and other obligations."

"Transfer of title? I thought the cars were already in my name?"

Sampson shot a nervous glance at Yael before hurrying to close the office door. She frowned and turned to Olivier for answers, jumping when she found him only inches from her face.

"You don't know?"

Leaning back, her frown deepened. "Know what?"

Olivier's look of incredulity was telling. "You've got to be kidding? What claim does this woman have? She doesn't even know who we are!"

"Sir, please? Ms. Piccirillo was to be briefed after the marriage was consummated. I will now provide the background she needs to make an informed decision. Miss, if you will."

She took the file from him and opened it, finding a death certificate inside atop the other paperwork.

"Let me start from the beginning, for both of your sakes. In the 1980s, a young royal approached me in this very office to request my services. She explained that she had run away with an American soldier and was now settling into her home, building a life here. But she had some doubts and worries that led her to believe she would not always be safe with the man she loved.

"Together, we set up several accounts and safe deposit boxes for her and her young son. She wanted him to have the option to go home to England and learn about his lineage. If that were to happen, and he decided to fulfill his duties as the Duke of Yorkshire, she wanted to be sure he had all the resources required to do so."

Yael felt sick all over again. "Duke…of Yorkshire?"

Olivier leaned her way once more and loudly cleared his throat. "Soon to be me."

"That remains to be seen. What I can tell you is that Mrs. Hill's remains were found wrapped in plastic in the rubble of the dojo. Based on the autopsy, it would appear she was strangled by her husband nearly two decades ago and placed in the wall of an addition in the upper room."

Yael blinked. The only addition in the upper room…was the bedroom. She looked at the attorney in horror; he was watching her already, a look of pity in his eyes.

Studying him as she steadied herself, she asked, "You were her attorney…any chance you want to be mine?"

Sampson bowed his head. "It would be an honor, miss."

"Marry me and you won't need an attorney," Olivier said with a wag of his brows.

Yael chuckled in spite of herself. "I would never marry someone so ridiculous."

"Well, sounds like you almost married my cousin. Couldn't be too far off, could I?"

"Exactly."

Olivier opened his mouth to speak, then snapped it shut and sat back with a puff.

Clearing his throat loudly, Sampson continued. "The reading of the will is a bit more complicated with the news of Mrs. Hill's death, but that is only if you two decide to fight over a few dozen heirlooms and two small estates. If you can come to an amicable agreement, we should be able to conclude our business rather quickly.

"Ms. Piccirillo, you and I can schedule a private session to review your options. You are under no obligation to accept or deny anything, regardless of what might be said otherwise."

Olivier placed his hand on his chest, an affronted look on his face. "Really, now, I would never!"

Yael rolled her eyes. "Give me some time to review this myself, I'll give you a call to set up the appointment. I assume you have a financial advisor who can attend?"

"Of course, miss."

"Well then, I think I've heard enough for today. Quite enough..." Standing and drawing herself up to her full height, she mustered the best royal voice she could and said, "Good day, gentleman."

CHAPTER TWELVE

Leaving the office with her head high, Yael felt proud of how she handled what now felt a lot like an ambush. She'd have to let her new attorney know that she didn't care for surprises.

"Madame!"

Groaning inwardly, she picked up the pace and hoped he would take the hint.

"Come on, now," Olivier said breathlessly as he fell in step beside her, "where are we headed?"

"I am headed to work."

Olivier stopped in his tracks. "Work?"

Yael kept walking. The man seemed harmless, but he was definitely annoying.

Very annoying.

"So *that's* why you're dressed like a barmaid?"

"Bartender," she corrected.

He made a rude sound. "Why would you want to do that?"

"I like people," she said simply, stopping at the corner to wait for the crossing signal to change.

"Oh, I see! All this money and no place to spend it?" He paused for a moment. "I've been there. But why serve people when you can hire them? You could be traveling — meeting people from all over."

Turning her head slowly, she gave him a look of disinterest and let out a long sigh.

He smiled and responded with a wink. "Look, if you don't know how to manage an estate, you really ought to find someone to help you."

"I believe you saw me do just that?"

"Pish posh, I say. That old wanker didn't do auntie any favors, what makes you think he'll be any help to you?"

Yael stepped into the street, quickening her pace and wondering what she could tell him to get him to leave her alone.

"Pity," he murmured. "I have a plethora of real estate experience and from what I can see, you've got land across the city. I'd be happy to help, no charge of course."

"No."

"You know, you could also give up now. Why deny our attraction?"

Yael made a face.

"Besides, if you still have an interest once we're married, I don't see a problem with allowing you to run certain aspects of the businesses."

"Oh?"

"Of course," he said with a bow.

"And what is it that you do for a living, Olivier?"

"Well, I'm British."

She burst out laughing.

"A sense of humor?" He clutched his chest. "Be still, my beating heart."

Yael let out another loud sigh, shaking her head as Margarita's came into view. "Look, mister, I'm flattered…I guess. But I'm involved, and I don't like you one bit."

"You say that now, poppet. But I assure you, I can be very charming."

"Oh, I don't doubt that. But I assure you, I don't want to be charmed. Here's a free tip — leave me the fuck alone. Now."

"Saucy."

Lips pursed, she continued. "Forever. And ever."

"How about this? I've got a tip for you. The property that held the martial arts studio has a larger footprint than it may seem. There is a lodge you'd have to demo, and a renter in the house on the corner. Building around it won't be much use, but…If you cleared the entire block, you could build up."

She followed his finger and looked at the sky. "Up?"

"Lofts, and a few businesses at the base of the building. The area is next to a private university and the students lack housing. That was my plan, but I give it to you now, no charge."

Yael stopped and turned to face him. "Are you telling me you already checked out the property?"

"Well, of course. Before you came along, I was the rightful heir."

Shit.

She hadn't considered that Xavier might have a family, let alone come from a royal line. The man was scum. And right now, she wasn't so sure she wanted such a fight; today was supposed to be the day she cut ties with him forever. Olivier's presence had already mucked things up. She needed time to think.

"This is my stop." She pointed her thumb into the bar. "Well, Olivier, it's been…an experience."

"The first of many, I hope?"

"The last and only, I hope."

"You know, I've never had a mar-ga-rita. This sign says you make the best in the world."

Yael stopped in front of the doorway, trying to think of a response clever enough to send him on his way. It would have to be a good one, too, judging by his sudden interest in margaritas. But the sound of heels click-clacking across the hardwood floor in the restaurant behind her caught her attention.

"Hey, bitch!"

Well, fuck me.

Olivier's eyes lit up with excitement. "And who might *this* vision of radiance be?"

Dropping her head into her hands, Yael tried her best not to scream. The banshee behind her screeched again.

"Bitch, I'm talking to you? Where is Xay?"

"Oh! Is she talking about my dear cousin?"

Stacey gasped and turned to face Olivier. "Cousin? Are you -"

"Lord Olivier Maxwell Hulley, the third, 15th Earl of Ravenscar."

Yael watched him bow, low, then take Stacey's hand and kiss her knuckle. When he stood, ever so slowly, staring into the woman's starstruck eyes, Yael took a step back in an attempt to fade out of view. But Stacey was studying Olivier intently, almost as if she didn't believe he were real.

What does she know that I don't? Yael wondered, her suspicions of him growing.

"And what is your name?" he murmured, giving her the once over.

"Stacey," she breathed out.

"Stacey," he whispered back, taking her hand into both of his. "I hate to be the one to tell you this, but…my dear cousin has lost his life in a terrible accident."

Yael snorted. They didn't seem to notice.

Stacey's face said she was shocked, but Olivier wasn't finished. He snaked his arm around her shoulders and pulled her in close.

"Now, now, don't cry! You're too pretty to cry. I'm in mourning, too. Would you like to come back to my penthouse suite and share our fondest memories over strawberries and champagne?"

Stacey nodded, her lips forming a pout as she let out a pitiful sniff.

"That's a good girl. How about we go on a trip in my private jet? My friend owns a very special island. I think we would have a wonderful time together, don't you?"

Stacey nodded again as Olivier steered her away from the bar and down the sidewalk, whispering into her ear all the way. Yael watched as his hand slipped down to the small of her back, then met his eyes as he turned to her and winked over his shoulder.

She couldn't help but chuckle.

It really was just about the money to Stacey, and Olivier obviously had plenty. Yael wouldn't be surprised if Stacey knew all about Xavier's royal family. Olivier would likely relish the attention.

Problem fuckin' solved!

Here she was, starting to detest the man…and now she'd never see either of them again. She didn't care to thank him.

"Good fucking riddance."

CHAPTER THIRTEEN

J oe tossed his pen onto the desk and sat back in his chair.

"Guys, this isn't working."

Clancy let out a long sigh. "When you're right, you're right. I'm stumped."

"This whole week has been shit," Weaver said, annoyed. "Twiddling our fucking thumbs."

"Alright, alright," Joe replied, recognizing the ticking time bomb sitting across from him. "Last file and we'll all go home."

Weaver picked up the file and groaned.

"Do we have to?" she whined.

"I told you, we should have done this one first."

Clancy caught the cheese puff Weaver threw at him and tossed it into his mouth with a crunch.

"First, last, let's just get it done," Joe offered, hoping to quell the bickering before it started. "Honestly, I think we need a clear board."

"I agree," Weaver said softly, surprising him.

Usually, she was her *most* disagreeable self after being stuck at her desk for weeks on end. Most of the cases they had been working since he returned were stalled out, but the local serial killer file left them gridlocked every time they touched it. There had been no movement since last month, when neighbors reportedly saw two people fleeing the scene of a gruesome crime near the stadium. Unfortunately, a downpour washed away much of the evidence from outside the home. Inside was another story.

Joe watched as Clancy pulled a whiteboard down from a slot in the ceiling and wiped it clean. They had turned this profile upside down numerous times, but without new information to work with, they had no other option than to try again. Clancy finished writing down the dates and the victims' known affiliations, then turned to look at Joe.

"Pull up the map, Weave."

With a few clicks on her laptop and a press of a button, the projector fan whirred on and a wide map of the Tampa Bay Area appeared on the wall. Joe signaled for Clancy to join them, and for a long while, they all stared in silence. When he was ready, Joe initiated the mastermind session.

"Weaver?"

Snapping out of her daze, she sat up and looked at Joe. Reluctantly coming to her feet, she clomped over to the board and picked up a marker.

"The pattern says the unsub might live somewhere between Westshore and Nuccio. Based on this cluster, I'd say our next move is to pin down income levels."

"There isn't much to go on," Clancy reminded her.

Joe stroked his chin. The long oval Weaver drew over the map covered a lot of different neighborhoods, all with mixed incomes. Even in South Tampa, where he lived, it was normal to find million dollar homes and run down rentals on the same street. And lately, he was starting to wonder if their killer was even local at all.

She paced back and forth in front of the map, studying it as she tapped her front teeth with her fingernail.

Capping the marker, she shrugged. "Fine, let's just make a note. I'm willing to bet he's got money, and if that's the case...he probably lives on like, Davis Island or maybe in Hyde Park? Now, if he's low-income or underemployed...the best central location would be either West Tampa or Ybor."

Joe shook his head. "That's all well and good — *if* he's local. But if these are mob hits, he'll have the money to fly in and out."

Tossing his pen, Clancy said, "If we're going with the mob angle, then I've got a lot more questions."

"Like what?"

Clancy sat back, tilting his head from side to side as he weighed the air with his hands. "My main beef? Why would any mafioso want to bring this kind of attention to themselves?"

"I asked the same thing," Weaver said. Joining them at the table, she poked the file as she continued. "Organized crime has changed a lot over these last few decades — especially in Tampa — but this part of the life certainly hasn't. There is one reason a crime family would make *this much* noise. Someone is trying to make a statement."

Clancy shot her a tired look. "The only chatter we heard anything about is now null and void."

Joe frowned. "Why?"

Weaver grinned and leaned in to explain.

"There were these brothers — the Rizzoli's. All three of em...dead!"

"What was their deal?"

She shrugged. "Rumor had it they were planning some kind of take over. Their grandpa was the *capo di tutti capi* around here for decades, but that particular crime family was edged out in the 90s. With those three gone, they're *all* dead now."

"So, why were these guys on our radar?"

"Uhr -"

Clancy grinned as Weaver popped one cheese puff too many into her mouth.

"I've got it, Weavey. Unit 2 was investigating them after their names came up on a few human trafficking watchlists. Everyone was worried that the remaining syndicates would get involved, but they realized the Rizzoli's weren't on the inside."

"So they *weren't* goodfellas?"

Weaver cut in. "No, no, they were definitely organized. But they didn't seem to be a part of anything local, even though they all grew up in Ybor. So, get this! Earlier this year, the youngest brother dies in like, a gang fight, or something like that? And then the two older brothers were found out in a trailer burnt to a fucking crisp."

Joe smiled at Weaver's enthusiasm. She loved a good story. "I still don't get how these guys are connected?"

Clancy sat up. "They were on *another* list."

"A hit list," Weaver said dramatically.

"And more than half our victims are on that list."

"What list?" Joe asked, still wondering what they were on about.

Weaver leaned back and crossed her arms. "Unit 2 has access to an enforcer hotline. It's pretty ingenious the way the whole thing works. First, somebody has to order a kill; a higher-up in the organization will call the number and leave the information. Then, the operator reroutes the order to a hitman. It's like a dial-a-hit switchboard. The youngest brother I mentioned? He was placed on a list a couple hours after he was already dead. The older brothers were on there, too."

"None of them matched the signature, though?"

"No," they said in unison.

Staring at them both, Joe shook his head. "I'm gone for a few months and you guys go off the deep end."

"You were gone a lot longer than that!"

Joe grimaced, patting Weaver's hand in apology. "So…"

"So, if we look at that list and our victimology, the brothers were the odd men out. They might be the key to this whole case."

Clancy made a face. "Or, they might not matter at all. The point is, they stand out on that list as the only other victims that match our victimology. Everyone else is either a perfect fit — and a victim — or they have no connection whatsoever. The Rizzoli's stand out, but no one can figure out why."

Joe looked at the ceiling. "So…"

"So, if our guy is just a hitman, it's not our case," Clancy said, brows raised.

"Ah."

Weaver's eyes glazed over as she stared at the file. "We were relying a lot on the Rizzoli evidence. We thought the case would close with them. Then we got the call about the scene by the stadium."

Lifting his arms to shake loose his sleeves, Joe rested his head in his hands and eyed the ceiling. "Okay, I think I'm understanding. You were banking on the Rizzoli's and the hitman angle in the hopes of being taken off the case."

"Right, because they were trying to take over," Weaver nodded.

"So…"

She threw up her hands. "So, obviously our guy is still out there. And if there's no war — no takeover — why not just send in a cleaning crew?"

Joe bit his lip. It did make sense. It would do a crime syndicate very little good to bring this much scrutiny to their dealings. These kind of groups specialized in premeditated murder and disappearing people. On the contrary, their killer wasn't just messy — he was asking for attention.

Although more than half of the victims had suspected or known ties to the Italian mafia, every single one had a criminal history. That alone *screamed* vigilante.

"Seems like we're back to the twisted vigilante theory?"

Clancy made a face. "Weaver?"

She shook her head. "There's no such thing. That's a serial killer."

"Right now, we need a motive," Joe said thoughtfully.

"He's a sick bastard," Weaver tossed out.

"Says who?"

Clancy and Weaver both frowned.

"Hey," Joe grinned, "I mean who says he's a *he*?"

Weaver shrugged. "I wouldn't want to meet the woman capable of this."

Thinking of Yael, Joe asked, "What would her motive be?"

"Man-hater?" Clancy quipped through a mouth full of Twizzlers. "Never mind, I forgot about these two."

They all looked at the photos of the only women in the pile and shook their heads. Discussions surrounding gender usually ended quickly. None of them had ever heard of a case like this with a female unsub; the woman with the capacity to pull these things off would have to be as tall and strong as a man. Impossible? No. Highly unlikely? They were willing to bet on it.

"Alright," Joe tried again, "what about the statement from the neighbors last month? Are we sure we're not dealing with a partnership?"

"I don't know, boss. I still think we're looking for a witness, not another killer."

Standing, Joe walked to the board and stared at the map. "Something about this profile still doesn't feel right. We're missing something here. Why not shift our perspective and try another angle?"

"What do you suggest?"

Yael flashed into his mind again. He pictured her the night they met, aiming her gun at him with a perfect grip and stance. This wasn't the first time he'd thought of her during a mastermind meeting, but her name seemed to be at the tip of his tongue tonight. He needed to clear his head, and so did his team for that matter. He stood and closed the file.

"We're going to take the weekend and explore a few new dynamics. Perhaps we are dealing with a strong, lone female. Maybe it's a duo — perhaps a submissive finds and kills the victim and a dominant bleeds them. Whatever you can come up with. On Monday, I want three potential profiles from both of you. And no more Rizzoli stories!"

OCTOBER

CHAPTER FOURTEEN

Frederico was in a testy mood. A full month of meticulously planning his outfit and procuring his accessories had ultimately led to a let down. All night, he'd heard *Blade* this and *Shaft* that. All night, he'd looked at people like they were idiots — only to have them laugh in his face and take his picture anyway. If one more person asked him who he was supposed to be, he was going to lose it.

Checking his watch, he wondered if he should head home once he finished packing up. The owner of the nightclub had promised him *twice* now that he would stay out of the server room, but it seemed he just couldn't help himself. Hopefully, after tonight's fiasco, he would learn his lesson.

Guavaween was one of Ybor's biggest celebrations of the year, and tonight was the 25th anniversary of the longstanding parade and street party. The main costume contest was only an hour away, but the Gaybor crowd held their own drag show and competition every year after the parade ended. The promoters of this event were lucky he was just down the strip at Margarita's when their system went out, or they would have lost even more business.

Yaya and Joe were successfully grating on his nerves, being unnervingly cute as she worked the busy bar. He liked Joe a lot more than he ever did that bastard Sensei, but he still didn't want to see his cousin making googly eyes every five seconds. And as nice as Joe was, the moment Frederico shook his hand he couldn't help but remember the man was a Fed. He didn't look like one, talk like one, or act like one…and that made him even more dangerous.

He was going to have to talk to Yael sooner than later, because there was *no way* she had thought things through. She was far too comfortable with the man. Didn't she understand that one wrong move could have her locked up for life?

And how long does she think she can lie to Joe?

The database Frederico was building to monitor the trafficking activity in the area was almost complete. He would be ready to show her how it worked in the next few weeks, so he could try to voice his concerns then. Hopefully, she would hear him out when she saw how serious he was taking their joint venture.

If she shows up this time…

Last month, Frederico found an online forum for hackers. Last week, he figured out how to tap into ViCAP. This morning, he located the girls Yael had freed from the sex dungeon *and* the forensic files from the trailer. He was itching to share all this with Yaya, but she barely came around anymore.

"Oh, thank God!"

Swinging around towards the door, Frederico was shocked to come face to face with the woman of his dreams. Her slim build, pert breasts, and perfectly toned muscles were everything he'd ever imagined. Well, she was shorter in person, but now that he saw her here…

Is this real?

"Sorry," she whispered softly, mouth agape as she fanned her face in the cool air.

He couldn't speak, couldn't form the words to ask her if she did, in fact, exist.

For the last decade, all he wanted was Mystique. Sure, she was fictional and straight out of a comic book, but what did that matter? After years of defending her as the perfect character — and arguing that she would be the best lay in the Marvel comic universe — she could be likened to his secret girlfriend. He knew it was... irrational. But that didn't stop him from talking about her like she was real.

Maybe there's a gas leak, he thought, his heart racing wildly. *I gotta get outta here.*

"Are you...Morpheus?"

Frederico looked down at his deep violet trousers, wondering if it were possible for her to identify the color in the dim light. He cleared his throat, but nothing came out. This beautiful beast staring at him with her wild blue eyes and painted blue skin made him feel seen, and known.

Nose wide open...

Nodding, he pointed to his upturned collar and lapel.

She nodded back, slowly, biting her lip as a little moan escaped her.

Clearing his throat again, he tried to move his feet. He knew where he was. This woman was at a party in the heart of Gaybor! He wasn't about to get his hopes up.

She don't want you, man.

That reminder helped. A lot. He cleared his throat once more.

"How'd you get the paint to stay on?"

"What paint?"

Frederico groaned inwardly when he felt his dick jump in his slacks. He knew she was just a normal woman, that Mystique was not real…but damn.

Smiling up at him, she bit her lip.

"Just kidding. Clear sealant."

"Looks…real."

With those eyes and a body like hers, he was grateful for the blue barrier keeping his thoughts in the realm of fantasy. But the radiant smile that lit upon her face revealed straight, bright white teeth and a dimple in her left cheek…and Frederico loved dimples.

"Double damn."

"Seriously," she breathed back.

Head cocked, his eyes flared as he pondered her meaning. After all, here *he* was at a Gaybor club…and *he* wasn't gay…

"Did you know Morpheus' character was derived from the Greek god of dreams?"

Frederico smirked. "Yeah."

"Oh."

He grinned. "Did you know Mystique was one of the first mutants on earth?"

"Yeah," she said, grinning right back.

"Whoa."

Scanning the room, she asked, "What are you doing in here?"

He glanced around. "Fixing another mess. Actually, fixed."

She took a step forward and looked down the hall of servers.

"All this for a nightclub?"

"All four clubs in this building are linked," he replied, dropping his bag into the chair next to him and standing in place beside her. "That whole row is for this club — they do a lot of drag shows. Pyrotechnics, all that."

"Uh huh."

When he caught her eyes, he realized they were on his lips. And she was close. So close.

Everything in him felt her calling him, beckoning him forward, but he couldn't bring himself to touch her. He was afraid she would disappear the moment he stretched forth his hand.

Chest heaving, she leaned in further, arching her back as if to limit the space between them. He could feel her breath on his neck, but he was barely breathing. All he could do was watch her watching him. And then —

"Oh, fuck it!"

She leapt into his arms, wrapping her legs about his waist and kissing him with the ferocity he would expect from his beloved Mystique.

He wasted no time sliding his hands across her skin to grip her ass and grind his hips into hers while they feasted on each other. She was smooth, but the paint on her skin gave it an otherworldly feeling that drove him over the edge.

He stepped towards the door, closing and locking it swiftly as she made her way down his neck. Never in his life had he felt such a need; every second of pleasure was equally agonizing, hard as he was.

Placing her down onto the desk, he released her and watched as she clawed at his belt and zipper. Though he wanted to lend a hand, he couldn't help but stare at her, study her. This was a memory he would savor for the rest of his life — if he didn't wake up first.

When he felt her grip his erection and deliver a soft, wet kiss to the tip, he let out a growl that shook the building. Pulling her to him, he kissed her again and again, an odd dissatisfaction growing in him knowing he could not taste her as she had him. He almost laughed at finding such a love-hate relationship with something as innocuous as blue paint.

She lay back until her head hit the wall and spread her legs wide. Her nipples were covered with some sort of circular sticker; the only item of clothing she was wearing was a thong also painted blue.

When she pulled it aside to reveal puffy, wet lips, his mouth dropped open. Every part of her body was covered in the blue paint, except a small sliver along her labia.

"Oh, fuck," he moaned, sliding his thumb over her clit.

When he pushed it back and saw pink, he shook his head and looked to the sky. He was pleased to learn that Mystique had a fat, gushy pussy, just like he always knew. And judging by the moaning and squirming he just brought out of her, she was going to be everything he dreamed of and more.

Looking her in the eyes as he slid inside, he knew he wouldn't last long. The woman wasn't just sexy, she was perfection.

"Fuck me till you come," she moaned.

When he felt her warmth wrapped around him, he hoped she wouldn't mind round two. Digging deep, he gave her his all and then some.

NOVEMBER

CHAPTER FIFTEEN

"Come in, young lady."

Yael rolled her eyes and pushed the heavy door closed, the loud click of the lock reverberating through the walls and into the surrounding tunnels. It had been some time since she was summoned before the Don, and she still had a sour taste in her mouth from their initial meeting earlier in the year.

Beneath the streets of Ybor City lay a system of tunnels dating back to the prohibition era. Locals and neighbors had varying levels of knowledge of the underground labyrinth, but most people believed the tunnels had been shut down in the 60s. Truth was, these tunnels were mafia territory — specifically, the Italian and Sicilian mafia run by the Don — and had been for generations. Only the Family — and trusted associates — knew of the various entry points around Ybor.

The tunnel office felt like a photo capture of days gone by. The gigantic space looked exactly the same as her first visit — minus the AV cart. The red, brown, and gold Oriental rugs — all with different designs and patterns — looked like they'd never been cleaned, shaken, or moved once they were put in place. The stench of stale smoke in the air combined with the dirty, cream-colored walls gave the room the feeling of a cigar lounge in desperate need of renovations. She wondered if it would ever change, if it ever had?

The Don was seated at his oversized cherry wood desk in the giant leather chair that made him appear smaller than he actually was. Yael noted that he looked older in this light, recalling how much younger he seemed in his marital bed when he wasn't wearing a tattered, ill-fitting suit.

His bald head shined in the dim yellow light centered above him as he flipped through the pages of a file folder. She wasn't sure of his mood, but hoped the frown on his face was there due to his surly nature, rather than her presence.

In the time that followed her first run-in with Vitto, the Don had only offered her three jobs. One was declined, as she was certain the mark was not one of hers; but the other two were offered within days of receiving a new vision. Both had gone off without a hitch.

Of course, she had also taken care of a few more personal kills, all of which came through with perfect clarity. Things had been quiet on her front, and Vitto was utterly silent. She was beginning to think she'd made a bigger mess of all this than she should have.

The Don put the folder down and motioned for her to have a seat.

"I'm sorry to say this, but we're gonna have to make a few changes until this shit clears up."

The color drained from her face. "What happened?"

The Don gave her a long, hard look. "The entire Family has been fighting about how to handle this honorably."

"Honorably for who?"

"I know you don't understand this, but Vitto comes from a long line of men just like him. Men who have given up *their* lives so that *we* may live."

Yael snorted. "Fucking noble."

"Ahh," the Don waved a hand dismissively. "It's all politics, believe you me."

He eyed her warily before continuing. "You know, for years I thought you were some kind of mole. Can I trust your loyalty?"

"To myself?" She snorted again. "Abso-fucking-lutely."

"Yeah, yeah." He sat back in his chair and rubbed the bridge of his nose. "Well, I think the Family might be dealing with some kind of infiltration. My cousin called me from Taormina yesterday — told me he heard through the grapevine that my statements are being relayed to Vitto."

"Who would do something like that?"

The Don shook his head. "Could be anyone. Everybody has their reasons, right?"

Yael shifted uncomfortably in her seat. "What's changing?"

"I would say 'hand in your gun' but I believe you bring those from home."

She didn't know what to think. Deep down, underneath her disdain for the man and all things mafia, she really enjoyed the work she did for the bar. More importantly…

"How does that stop him from finding me?"

The Don gave her a hard look. "It doesn't."

Tilting her head to the side, she couldn't help but raise a brow in question.

The Don rested his elbow on the desk and scratched his chin. "Why didn't you tell Johhny what happened when you took out Lo Mascio?"

She stared at him blankly, trying to recall which of her last marks he was referring to. When the memory came flooding back, her cheeks were red hot.

"Uh huh. That's what I thought," he grumbled. "He saw you, didn't he?"

Yael didn't answer. The very notion of Vitto's eyes meeting hers through the window brought an unexpected physical response. Heart racing, she did her best to push the intense fear from her mind.

"Johhny did the research, kid. All the bodies you took out, Vitto bled out — save the Rizzoli's. I'm thinking he went in, took the pictures for us, then left the damn bodies in the mess. The son of a bitch has us wrapped up with the fucking Feds."

Yael blinked. "Feds?"

The Don nodded. "Ah, don't worry about them."

She nodded with him, but she was shaking inside. What would the Don say if he knew about Joe? And what would Joe say if he knew about the Don? Shoving the thoughts deep, *deep down*, she swallowed and tried to focus on what he was saying.

"Besides, there's a chance they'll do your job for you and take him out. Until then, you're off the payroll."

"Is that all he wanted?" she wondered aloud.

"I could give a shit what he wants! This is chess, not checkers."

Wishing she knew more about both games, Yael decided she didn't enjoy being a pawn either way. "So, that's it then?"

"What? Hell no. I know a good employee when I see one."

"Oh."

"We're finally ready for the big launch. You're gonna be my bar manager."

Yael laughed. The first time she came to this office, *that* was the position she had been expecting to be hired onto. She clapped her hands together and leaned forward. "It's about damn time."

"I should say the same thing to you," the Don retorted. "Every time your name comes up in conversation, I see dollar signs."

"I'm gonna need a raise."

A loud snort escaped him. "You've been working off tips since you started."

"Yeah, that's true. So I guess I should say, I want a salary. *A big one*."

"Geez," he replied, rubbing the bridge of his nose. "You give an inch…"

"You ready for the name?"

"Of what?"

"The bar," she snipped out. "We're gonna call it 'The Lieu'."

"You wanna call my bar the fucking toilet?"

She grinned. "Yep."

"Explain."

Yael stood and opened her arms wide, trying to paint a picture. "I can see it now — a big neon sign behind the stage."

"What stage?"

"Bruno is gonna build me one. And above the bar, we'll have a banner that reads '*L'Unione Italiana Easy Underground*'."

"'The Lieu'," he repeated thoughtfully.

"'The Lieu'," she whispered. "We're gonna have the best kept secret in town. Theme nights, lounge singers, happy hours, the whole nine."

The Don was giving her an odd look.

"What?"

"I don't like it," he said gruffly. "You've got six months."

Yael squealed.

"Well, that's nice."

She stuck her tongue out and started towards the door.

"Uh, young lady? We're not finished."

Clearing her throat, she reluctantly returned to her seat in front of his desk. Doing her best to curb her sarcasm, she forced a smile through her smirk and waited.

He wasn't amused. "Take a look at this."

She studied the map he handed her. The yellowing paper was old and heavily marked up, but it didn't take long for her to realize what she was seeing. Her eyes landed on a street labeled 7th Avenue.

"The strip?"

"And the tunnels. This is just a piece of the puzzle, but you should see it." He pointed at the edge of the map to a small arrow. "We reinforced those tunnels about fifteen years ago. Rats were coming in from the entrances here and here, and we had no use for the Port anymore. Too many eyes."

"Giuseppe," Yael whispered softly, tracing her finger along the map as she tried to find their current location.

"He had a stack of these maps in the trunk of his car."

Yael remembered the oldest Rizzoli brother's passionate speech about taking over the city — and how he wanted to start with the tunnels. If only she had thought to pick his brain before she pulled the trigger with her gun barrel in his ear…

The Don crossed his arms. "We have no way of knowing if he shared these with anyone. So far, all of the boards covering the entrances are still intact, as far as my guys can tell. This trafficking operation was a lot bigger than they let on, and everything seems to point back to Lorenzo and Giuseppe."

She bit her lip, wondering if she should tell him what she found at the Rizzoli's trailer of terror. "There were girls there."

"Excuse me?"

She blanched. "At the trailer. I…helped them escape."

"For fuck's sake, kid. Are you fucking kidding me?"

"Hey, man! You don't get to make me feel bad for saving someone's life!"

The Don stared at her, fuming. "Listen to me and listen good. You are a part of this Family now, like it or not. You slip up and our entire fucking operation goes to shit. You wanna save a life? Save me. Save Johhny."

"Neither of you needs saving."

"How would you know what we need?"

Yael frowned. She had never heard him sound so…sad. "I just want to help you find out what the Rizzoli's were up to."

"Why, so you can go play vigilante?"

"Yup," she said plainly.

He stared her down for a long while. "According to one of my informants, the Rizzoli's were looking to hire someone to take me out. I can't be too sure that wasn't already in motion or who all was in on it. Start at the Port."

"Okay."

"We pay good for information around here, kid. Make sure you bring it to me first this time. No more secrets."

CHAPTER SIXTEEN

Yael ran up the steps two at a time, the anxiety of the night finally having set in now that she was almost ready. When she moved in three months ago, she'd been worried about being so close to Joe day-in and day-out. What she had not considered is that they were both loners who had a tendency to throw themselves into their work — and that wouldn't change overnight.

Joe and his team worked cases all over the region, and she was now the General Manager of two different bars in Ybor. Though he had a key to her place, he never used it. She had a key to his house now, too, but she only used it to get in at night when he was already sleeping. If Joe was in town, they slept together, and she shifted the schedules at work to give them time for breakfast or dinner. But what they lacked was the intimate alone time she was beginning to think would never happen.

So last month, when Joe's boss forced him to take a week off, she was thrilled. Because the one thing she still hadn't told him, the one thing she wanted — no, needed most of all was finally going to happen. She refused to be a 23-year-old virgin, and there wasn't much time left to prevent that.

Tossing her long, thick hair up into a loose bun, she turned on the shower and examined the outfit she'd hung on the back of the bathroom door. Yael hoped it would give her an air of sophistication and prowess, though she couldn't help but feel like a fraud. The black lace bra and g-string panty set included a garter, which was wrecking her nerves all day. She never enjoyed donning all the lace and ribbons, especially since she thought lingerie was a big waste of money. But according to stories from the bar, most men appreciated their women dressing up from time to time.

The one thing she was banking on tonight was Joe's inability to resist her. On a couple of occasions since she moved in, she put her best foot forward and worked hard to earn a ravishing from the man after a long, stressful week. But in spite of their passionate kisses, there was an awkwardness between them. She had never seen him naked, and he hadn't seen her bare all either.

Sliding her fingers down her waist, she wondered if Joe would find her too firm in some places, and not firm enough in others. Her taut, muscular figure was accentuated by her large breasts, wide hips, and full, round bottom. Some men liked a little more ass, some wanted more up top, and others still wanted a woman with just enough to hold onto all around. Though she hated to think about it, some preferred a woman who was much softer than she would ever be. Which one was Joe?

This is stupid.

As much as she hated questioning herself, eavesdropping on her cousin's locker room talk for the last five years had led to a lot of insecurities. Shaking the thoughts from her mind, she hurried into the shower.

After spending the day cleaning, whipping up simple hors d'oeuvre, and grabbing the rest of the ingredients for their Thanksgiving meal tomorrow, she hadn't left herself much time to do anything else. Joe would be at her door in less than an hour, and she needed at least half that to get dressed and do her makeup. Peering out of the shower, she decided to forego the cocktail dress and wear her black silk robe instead.

"No misunderstandings tonight," she mumbled, scrubbing her body with the loofah. Bringing a shampoo bottle to her lips she sang, "*Let's get it on…ah, baby…*"

YAEL PLACED her glass on the coffee table and leaned forward to play with one of Joe's dreadlocks. She watched his eyes wander, lingering on the smooth golden skin of her calf. He had been staring at the openings in her robe all night, and she was enjoying every minute of the admiration.

She could tell he was sensing her mood. His voice was low and deep, and he'd gone for the second glass of wine without hesitation. But as usual, he made no advances toward her beyond the usual kisses.

This kiss, this kiss…

Yael smiled. All day long she was hearing love songs in her head — some she didn't even know she knew. Yes indeed, tonight was the night she'd been waiting for.

"Kiss me," she whispered.

Joe grinned and pulled her into his lap.

Sliding her arms around his neck, she lifted her lips to his and braced herself for the spark of magic. And it was good that she did, for the wine gave them all they needed to melt the very instant they touched.

She was no longer a novice at kissing, and no longer so nervous during these intimate moments. Joe was the only man who had ever kissed her, and now she knew exactly how to kiss him back. Each time his lips touched hers, a reaction neither could explain would occur. But tonight felt different — far more intense.

The sensation between her legs stirred up a whirling in her belly that left her breathless. Floating like a butterfly, she moaned into his mouth as the ecstasy rolled through her senses and she neared the fiery peak. She almost gave in but —

"We need…more wine."

Joe stared at her as she pulled herself away and jumped to fill their glasses. When she turned to face him from the kitchen, he was frowning at her with his hand on his chest looking affronted.

She cleared her throat. "So, what do you think of the house?"

He shook his head, eyes narrowing suspiciously. "Looks staged."

Yael stopped herself from sticking her tongue out at him by downing the glass of wine she poured herself. "Good — that's what I was going for. Have I showed you the bedroom?"

Joe waggled his brows. "Come to think of it, no, you have not."

Giggling, she beckoned for him to follow her and started towards the stairs. When she saw him running her way from the corner of her eye, she burst out laughing and ran.

But he was quick, wrapping her up in an embrace from behind and kissing his way down her neck before giving her a slap on the rump.

Doing her best to wiggle just right, she climbed the steps slowly.

Deep breaths, she reminded herself. *Just say it.*

When they reached the top of the steps, she walked to look out the window and watch the water lap at the sand on her private beach. She imagined them there, together, making love in the sand under the stars. Where everything else in her life made her feel numb, he had made it possible for her to dream again.

Turning to pull him closer, she did her best to formulate the right words. Unfortunately, all she could blurt out was, "Why haven't we ever had sex?"

Eyebrows lifting slowly, he looked at her and smiled. "We haven't?"

She shook her head, eyeing him curiously.

"We should remedy that immediately," he murmured.

Before she had time to respond, he was kissing her. She felt her back press into the glass as he devoured her, then licked his way to her neck and back up to her earlobe to plant another kiss.

"Joe!"

He chuckled, knowing exactly what his lips were capable of. Ignoring her plea, he dropped to his knees and kissed his way across her belly.

"Oh, fuck," she moaned, feeling her legs give way as she vaguely wondered if the window would hold.

When he planted a firm kiss atop her mound, she reached for his head, then his shoulders, trying to steady herself. Another chuckle brought her back to reality, and she found herself in his arms being carried to her bed.

"No kissing," she begged, "just this once, please!"

A boisterous laugh escaped him and she covered her face in shame.

"Alright," he said through a wide smile as he dropped her on the bed, "just this once."

"Oh, God," she blurted out, relieved. "Joe, I want you so bad!"

He moaned in reply, leaning in to kiss her. Stopping inches from her lips, he closed his eyes and shook his head. "I don't know if I can stop myself."

Sucking her lower lip into his mouth, he released it with a slight pop.

Yael couldn't blame him. If he wanted her as much as she wanted him, she would probably slip up soon.

"Just…fuck me."

His face went slack as he searched her eyes. She knew instantly she had hurt him, she just didn't know how.

"I'm sorry," she whispered, kissing him sweetly. "I'm sorry, I want you. I need you."

Exhaling softly, he kissed her back and nodded. Standing and pulling her up with him, he began to undress. She swallowed nervously, watching him unbutton his shirt and avoiding his gaze. When he reached forward to untie her robe, she flinched.

He stopped, eyes searching hers again.

She tried to play it off with a nervous giggle, reaching forward to slide his shirt off his shoulders. Distracting herself with the whispy expanse of hair on his broad chest, she bit her lip wantonly and arched her back. Pressing herself into him, she snaked her fingers down his torso and grazed her hands across his hard member.

"Oh."

Joe smiled at her, head shaking slightly as he unbuckled his belt. Yael licked her lips in anticipation, tugging at his zipper as he unbuttoned his pants. Slipping both thumbs into his waistband, he pulled his pants and briefs down over his hips until his thick, bouncing dick sprang forth.

"Oh!"

Yael stared open-mouthed as she felt her nerve slipping away. When she glanced up and found him watching her with an expression of amusement on his face, her eyes widened in surprise. But his burst of laughter broke the spell.

She was confused. "How is *that* supposed to fit *in here*?"

Tears in his eyes, Joe tried to curb his humor. "I'm sure we'll find a way."

Walking her back to the bed, he kissed her and gave her a little push, then fell onto his side next to her. Seconds later, he was licking along the edge of her bra and running his hand over her thighs. When he found her g-string already soaked, he dropped his head onto her shoulder.

"Jessum peace," he murmured, "pum pum so wet!"

"Joe, please!"

He popped his head up and looked at her, his own surprise apparent.

"Please? I can't wait anymore."

Shaking his head, he groaned and lifted himself up to pull her panties down. Exhaling sharply as he looked her over, he climbed on top of her and pushed his head between her lips with a deep, guttural moan.

Yael was on edge, but it didn't matter. Everything would be different in just a few seconds. Bracing herself for the pain she'd been dreading for years, she closed her eyes and waited.

For a few seconds, she felt Joe sliding his head up and down, pushing it against her clit each time he reached the top. But then, she felt nothing. Turning to face him, she realized her mistake a moment too late.

"What's all this?"

"Hmm?"

"No 'hmm'," he said sitting back onto his knees. "What you making faces for?"

"I - I don't," she stammered, unsure of how to recover. "Don't you want me?"

"You know I do. Explain yourself."

Swallowing, she sat up and covered herself with the nearest pillow.

Joe shook his head and climbed out of bed.

"Wait," she cried, "I'm sorry, I -"

Ignoring her, he leaned to pick up his pants and started to redress.

"Joe, please?"

When he didn't answer and picked up his shirt, she launched out of bed.

"Joe, I'm sorry! I've never -"

"Aha!"

Yael gasped.

"I knew it," he insisted, looking smug. "Now, explain."

"Explain?"

He crossed his arms, waiting.

"Um...well...I'm a - a -"

"A virgin," he said pointedly, clearly annoyed.

"Well, yes," she snapped, scooping up her robe. "I'm a 22-year-old virgin."

"Why the hell you didn't tell me this?"

"Because of this!" she exploded.

"What?"

"You don't want me now!"

"What!" Joe burst out laughing.

Yael felt the sting of tears before the lump in her throat as she remembered exactly *who* taught her *that* about men.

The bastard...

"You crying?"

She tried to stop, but her quivering lip gave it all away.

"Woman," he said softly, only a slight irritation in his voice now, "come."

Picking her up once more, he carried her to bed and held her while she quietly released her embarrassment and shame. Though she desperately wished she could tell him everything Xavier had done to her, she knew he would see her differently. And if he ever found out *who* Xavier was to *her*...

"Yael," he whispered, nudging her with his nose. "How could you do this?"

She felt a piece of herself break. The man really had no idea...

"How could you do this to me, knowing how I feel about you?"

Burying her face into his chest, she shook her head.

"I want to love you, woman. I do. I dream of it all the time... but I am in no rush. And you don't have to be either."

Sighing, she nodded and let out a little sniff in reply.

"Wipe your face," he said sternly, handing her the corner of her flat sheet. "We need to make this a good memory."

"How? This is just dreadful."

"Not for me," he retorted hotly. "So let me change that for you."

And with that, he kissed her to sleep.

CHAPTER SEVENTEEN

J oe snapped his phone shut and sighed. Clancy thought there'd been a break in a case, but it turned out to be a false alarm. Slipping his cell back into his pocket, he grabbed the glass Yael handed him and forced a smile.

Things had been awkward today, which was unfortunate. This was supposed to be their first family holiday together, and the day had still been nice, but it wasn't perfect. He wasn't the type of man to expect perfection from others — though he often aimed for it. Still, who could blame him? Life with this woman was the closest to perfection he'd ever known. For them, an awkward moment was hell, knowing what they were missing.

And today, his woman proved to him she was even more perfect than he already knew. Her mind was sharp and her heart was pure, and it showed as they worked together to create their multicultural feast from scratch. Though they ditched the turkey, they spent the day jumping between cookbooks: fresh baked naan with garlic and cilantro would accompany the bright green hariyali chicken from India; ground lamb and rice with herbs were stuffed into grape leaves to create Greek dolmades; and though their try at pierogi's didn't look at all appetizing, the potato dumplings still tasted delicious. He thought she was crazy to choose *eleven* new recipes, but she'd planned everything out and had no problem working through the issues as they came.

Last night, he'd learned more about her than he knew he was missing. Her face was timeless, but the depth of her mystery gave her a sense of wisdom beyond her years. To learn she was only twenty-two made so much sense to him, but also none at all. To learn she was a twenty-two year old virgin? No, a woman like his woman shouldn't exist.

His wife, prim and proper as she was, had not been a virgin. And at twenty-two, she was far more immature and far less industrious than the woman before him. Not that he was comparing. In truth, the two had little in common.

The reality was, Yael was somehow everything he could ever want in a woman while simultaneously being like no woman he'd ever known. On paper, she was his dream girl; it was like he designed her himself. Then again, the more he learned, the more she seemed…*too perfect*.

He had never met a virgin who didn't act virginal. Stranger still was that she hid her virginity from him and even tried to give it to him in secret. Admittedly, there was always something off about her behavior when they shared their intimate moments. The hesitance, the nervous excitement, all of it made sense now. But hiding it?

No, there was something wrong here and he knew it.

And he hated that every time he thought about it, his mind went straight to his case. As a criminal psychologist, he understood the reason behind it. But it bothered him to no end that there was no way to put a stop to it.

You could always ask.

Asking Yael questions was tricky. And since she didn't ask much of him, it left very few openings to do so naturally. Joe shifted uncomfortably, doing his best to keep his expression neutral.

"What's the matter?"

He smiled. *At least she knows me…*

"I saw you check your phone, mister."

"I know, I know," he mumbled. "No more phone tonight."

"Promise?"

"I promise. Now kiss me."

Taking no time to think, she put down her glass and took his, then threw her leg over his lap and straddled him. He didn't move, choosing instead to watch her take the lead.

The look in her eyes was enough to make him melt; he loved to gaze into her soul, loved the connection they shared by sight alone. He would often lose himself in the deep, brown pools of mystery, sometimes imagining he was siphoning her secrets through his stare.

Her golden skin was only a few shades lighter than his, but he found it just as mesmerizing, the way it captured the glimmer of the sun or the light of the fire. Her crowning glory was her long, silky mane of luscious black curls; even now, he found it difficult to keep his hands out of it.

Most of all, Joe loved the way she bit her lip, the way she looked at him just before she kissed him. And in the months since their first kiss, she learned to take her time and kiss him just so, bringing him to peaks unseen in all his experience. He had never felt more loved, more wanted by a woman.

This moment was no different, and soon he felt his need rising, felt a deep throbbing that beat in unison with his racing heart. When Yael's hands took his and placed them on her breast and buttock over her clothes, a flash of her lying naked beneath him on the bed the night prior caused him to groan.

Fingers creeping up his neck, she buried her hands in his hair, supporting his head as she thrust her tongue into his mouth. Vague wonderings about their first time together always crept into his mind when she kissed him so, but he was shocked when the dam burst at the thought of her lips elsewhere on his body.

He, too, had wondered why neither of them felt the need to push for more, but it was in these moments that he remembered. There was so much about their relationship he had trouble explaining, but the magic of their kisses could only be described as supernatural. The pleasure that coursed through his body when their lips touched was unreal.

Admittedly, a part of him was nervous to enjoy her on a deeper level. These orgasmic moments were so overwhelming that it was not uncommon for them to pass out. What would happen if he was inside her — or on top of her — and lost consciousness?

Joe was in a daze, eyes half open as he felt wave after wave of pleasure spread each time she planted a kiss here or there. From his cheeks, to his neck, to his collarbone, she gave him the feeling of being high, then higher with every passing moment. And when she finally stopped, snuggling into him and breathing softly in his ear, he felt himself overwhelmed with feeling once again.

"YAEL?"

She sat up in his lap and gave him a catlike smile.

"What was so special about last night?"

Smile fading, she sighed. "Just felt right, I guess."

Joe understood. It was the most time they'd spent together since she moved in. "We've had a lot of chances to, but I can see why you would say that."

Yael shrugged. "At least we talked about it."

"Did we?"

She cleared her throat. "I mean, yeah?"

"We haven't spoken all day…"

Sliding off his lap, she turned and stared at the dying fire. "I meant we talked about it last night."

Joe shook his head. This wasn't how this conversation was supposed to go. "Okay, you're right. How about now, you tell me something new."

"Like what?"

Trying his best not to press her, he thought of something simple. "Did you call your family for Thanksgiving?"

"I told you, I don't have a family."

"What about Fred?"

Yael blanched. "Oh, yeah…but, no. We don't really do holidays like that. Normally we just have a big party or I go to work."

"A party on Thanksgiving? My kind of function, eh? A lot of people come or just a few friends?"

"I told you," she said, frustration evident in the tension on her face, "I don't have any friends."

"Why you getting defensive, Yaya?"

She shook her head. "I'm not. You already know all this."

"Then tell me something I don't already know. What about school? No friends from high school or college?"

"I got my GED a couple years ago." Head hanging, she continued, "I thought about going to UF — that's where I got accepted — but I just can't see myself in a classroom anymore."

"See, that's something. I never knew any of that."

Standing and grabbing their wine glasses, she shook her head bitterly. "Honestly, Joe? What does it even matter?"

"Why are you so afraid to let me in, Yael?"

She frowned. "Maybe there just isn't anything to let you *in on*, Joe. The past is the past, and I don't like thinking about mine. And damn it, Joe! You are the only person in the world I feel comfortable with, why would I ruin it by talking?"

He watched her cross the living room and knew by her posture that he'd made her cry. *Again.* He knew it best to let her distract herself. Sure enough, he heard her turn on the sink to start the dishes.

No family?

No friends?

A hidden past?

Logic said this woman was up to something, but he'd thrown *his* out the window where *she* was concerned. One thing was for sure: he needed to figure out what was going on.

If these were his own insecurities or fears, it was wrong to keep projecting. She had every right to her privacy, and so did he. But sometimes, he felt like they were doing things backwards.

At times, being with Yael made him question his masculinity. He felt downright womanly in his uncertainty, trying to discuss *feelings.* Meanwhile, his woman was resorting to seduction and manipulation to get sex. Virgin or not, last night was a reminder that Yael had needs and he had to try to understand that, even now.

Don't do this man!

You know you're right — something is seriously wrong here.

Says who?

Maybe I'm the real problem?

Joe sighed.

No, he wouldn't let himself go down that road again. He was

man enough to admit that he cared, and he believed he deserved answers to simple questions. Life inside their bubble wasn't supposed to be so tense, and she would have to let her guard down eventually.

Maybe they *both* needed to slow down? Just as there was no rush for them to know each other physically, there was no rush to know each other mentally. Right?

Hell, if he was being honest, his latest caseload was enough to drive any man crazy. That had to be why he still found himself thinking about Yael when he worked the exsanguination case. The feelings he had, the doubts and questions…they wouldn't stop coming.

She'd yet to explain why she showed up at his house with a gun the night they met — or why she pulled it on *him*. Until she did, his brain would continue to try to make it make sense. If only she would talk to him. If only they had gone a little faster before slowing things down. His mind couldn't take the questions much longer.

You're just stressed, man. This is stress.

The glamorous nature of his new specialized team ebbed and flowed as the cases were closed. He had never worked this hard in his life, and he had to at least acknowledge that Yael didn't deserve to be misunderstood because he was having trouble coping.

He hoped it was just that.

CHAPTER EIGHTEEN

Yael was not in the mood. But unlike most people, the first place she went when she didn't want to deal with people was…work.

Years of working in the hospitality industry had taught her that people were oblivious and servants were invisible. Alone with her thoughts was one of the hardest places for her to be. Going to work gave her the distraction she needed, and tonight would be no different.

The Saturday after Thanksgiving was the official date for many of the annual rivalry games in college football. Though she didn't attend, the University of Florida was still her school of choice. After all, the idea of one day leaving for college was the only thing that got her through high school. She owed the university her life.

Even though she wasn't much into sports these days, she took her love of the Gators more seriously than she should. It was one thing she had in common with the common folk she served. And since the football team just lost to their rival, Florida State — and horribly at that — she knew *everyone* at the bar would have *something* to say.

Sadly, calling in was not an option when you requested the shift. Luckily, the thought of staying busy tonight made it worth it, even if she was facing unrelenting harassment.

Plus, she was only a block away now. And Joe was still at home for the weekend, so there was nowhere else to go.

Get a grip, it's just for the night.

She was trying to pretend that everything was fine; she'd never been very good at it. Being hard on herself? Sure. Hypercritical? Absolutely. But for the past two days, she repeatedly had to pull herself off the ledge. And once she did, her inner voice was right there to remind her just how foolish she was.

At least you're trying!

That was a good point, one she would do well to remember. When she wasn't being overtaken by invasive thoughts and frazzled nerves, Yael searched for new ways to cope with her self. Finding the motivation to come to work tonight was proof she was heading in the right direction.

Screams of joy sounded off across the strip. She smiled at the delayed shouts from behind her, where a particular bar was known for its crappy satellite signal. Wondering who was playing, she craned her neck to see into the bar as she approached the window. The SEC crowd was fairly rowdy but manageable — it was the ACC and BIG10 fans she couldn't stand. Then again, maybe she was biased...

"A vision of loveliness, dare I say it?"

You've got to be fucking *kidding me?* Yael's mouth dropped open in shock, then snapped shut.

"Don't look so surprised, darling," Olivier murmured.

Dressed to the nines in a tan suit, he held his jacket over his shoulder as he leaned against the door frame. His overlong, hawk nose was red at the tip, and his bulging, close-set eyes that held more than a hint of crazy in them were glassy and bloodshot. Though he wasn't conventionally handsome, he had the swagger of a very wealthy man, even drunk as he was.

Stepping out of the way of a customer, he tipped his imaginary hat, then leaned towards Yael and inhaled deeply.

"I knew it," he said softly. "Your scent haunts me."

Yael made a face. "Gross."

He reached for her hand, gripping it tightly when she tried to pull away. Brushing his lips across her knuckles, he smiled and bowed.

"I've been looking for you all weekend."

"Don't."

"You say that now…"

"I say it always. Forever. And ever."

Olivier tossed his head back and laughed. "Such a minx."

Casually throwing his arm over her shoulder, he steered her out of the doorway until she started to struggle. He wasn't phased.

"I heard about you, you know?" he said, his voice barely audible.

"Oh? How nice for you."

Whispering faintly, he elaborated. "I don't care what kind of woman you are, Ms. Picky, er…Ms. Peachy."

Yael's eyes widened.

"I had Stacey, and I still want *you*. Do you hear me? I want you bad, Peach."

Paralyzed, she caught the eye of one of the bouncers. Doing her best to signal for help, she tried to stop the tears from falling.

"Let me go," she grit out, the rage she needed finally pressing through.

"Never."

But he did let her go, just as two of her bouncers arrived in the doorway.

"Okay, buddy," Bear said, grasping his shoulder firmly, "let's call you a cab."

"That's quite alright, good man. My driver is waiting in the town car."

Turning to Yael, Olivier gave her a wink, tipped his imaginary hat again, and strolled cheerfully down the strip.

"You good, boss?"

Yael looked at Dallas and nodded slowly, still finding it strange that all her male employees now called her that.

"I'll be right in, guys."

Wiping her face and taking a few long, deep breaths, she heard Olivier's confession ringing in her ears.

I want you bad.

Yes, this was bad. She shook her head and hugged herself as a breeze sent chills up her spine.

"Bad, bad."

DECEMBER

CHAPTER NINETEEN

The Lieu's first open lounge night had gone off without a hitch, and Yael finally felt like she had a win on the board. It was obvious her role in the Family scheme was out, but she didn't really mind. Half of the people in the room were likely killers themselves, and most lived unsavory lives that were expected to come to a tragic end. The underground bar was becoming one place she didn't have to hide. It was a nice feeling.

Visiting the bar used to feel like walking into your uncle's unfinished basement where he happened to serve liquor. The upgrades made it a cozy space. Johnny told her the place reminded him of the old clubs up north, particularly the color scheme: the red and black fabrics were accented by silver and gold, and glass crystals hung from the chandeliers and lampshades. Newly restored oversized chairs and stuffed sofas were organized in a semicircle around the projector screen to create a makeshift cigar lounge. Bruno was able to get the old baby grand piano fixed, and it now sat across from the entrance adjacent the stage.

All over the bar, the ladies of the night claimed the few chaise lounges, posing provocatively as they awaited their lovers and johns. There was a smattering of strategically placed plush areas and secret corners for those lovers, as well as hidden business exchanges. The Lieu was made just for the riffraff — except here, they were royals.

Her night was over, but she was still riding the high as she made her way to the parking lot. Sliding into the driver's seat, she took a few moments to enjoy the satisfaction, smiling as she recalled the shock on everyone's face when little Rita got up to sing.

When Yael started the open lounge idea, she had hoped to find a few permanent fixtures for the new stage. Rita had something about her that was undeniable. The fact that she was a Family call girl — and a favorite at that — would bode well for her potential singing career *and* the books if she was willing to take the job.

Just as Yael opened her phone to shoot the girl a text, a flash of yellow sent her reeling. Pressing her wrists into her forehead, she squeezed her eyes shut against the pain.

"Fuck!"

The damned visions confused her still. Always varying in their intensity, they came when they pleased and often took everything out of her. Though she was getting better about opening her mind to the things she saw, they didn't happen frequently enough for her to practice.

Breathe, damn it!

She gasped but found no relief. Sitting back in her seat, she lifted her chest and tried again. Panic gripped her.

Oh, God!

She screamed. The pain was growing by the second. It felt like her mind was being ripped apart.

"Okay!" she sobbed, giving in as the blinding light broke through a barrier she could not see, only feel.

Suddenly, she was there.

Then, she wasn't.

"No!"

Gasping for breath, she shook her head mindlessly, refusing to see what she could not unsee.

"I can't!"

But deep down, she knew she would. And if the feeling she had was right, she would do it *now*.

Starting the car, she tore out of the lot with a sob as she raced towards 4th street. Though she had never seen the house she was headed to, it didn't matter. Moments before, she lived this. Her mind's eye had shown her every light signal, every street sign.

But when she blinked, she was already there.

"What the fuck?"

What was happening to her? No longer in Ybor, she found herself on the other side of the interstate.

Did I black out?

Looking at the clock, she was almost certain five minutes had passed. She stopped the car and stared at the small house, wondering if she'd already gone inside to do the deed. But when she reached to check her gun in the glove compartment, she knew the weapon hadn't been fired.

I blacked out!

Calm down.

I've never blacked out!

Calm the fuck down!

Yael tried breathing, but it wasn't working. And the harder she tried to remember what she had just seen, the less she was able to recall. Was the vision really so bad? She swallowed the lump in her throat and drove around the corner to park her car.

A few minutes later, she was tip-toeing along a wooden fence, following a feeling she hoped she'd read correctly. The tears were gone and the panic was subsiding.

She welcomed the numb.

The yellow and blue IKEA sign on the other side of the highway shone brightly, beckoning her forward as she made her way back to the shack. When she saw an open window, she froze.

What now? she wondered.

Adrenaline was flooding her system, but her gifts seemed to be failing her. Where was the *knowing*? Why did she have such an awful feeling in her belly?

Shaking her head, she crept toward the edge of the building and ducked under the sheet hanging from a clothesline. There was another sheet on the other side, blocking her from view.

Pulling her gun from her waist, she closed her eyes and tried to sense what to do next. The window seemed to call her name, but something about it also frightened her. And she couldn't remember if there would be a fight tonight…would he be waiting for her on the other side?

That's why you've got this.

She nodded. Tonight, she was going to shoot first. She was tired of all the questions.

But just as she took a step forward, she heard a sound.

Was it tree branch or maybe a possum? It *was* late enough for the rodents to be out rummaging around. And the house was only a few blocks from the Port, an area she frequently heard people complaining about due to all the rats.

Just a rat, just a rat.

She shook it off and adjusted her grip on the Walther P22,

realizing she was hurting herself. After years of doing things a certain way, she had to acknowledge these new visions would take some getting used to. And she had to admit, she'd become spoiled ever since she started working for the Don. Knowing she had backup was a luxury she lost when she did her own thing.

There was no more time to waste. The longer she stood here, the longer she would have to sit in her fear. Resolving herself to kicking every ass she encountered tonight — then hoping there wouldn't be more than one ass in the tiny house — she looked up to the sky in silent prayer and made her way to the window.

It didn't make a sound as she lifted it the rest of the way open. Only at the last push did it let out a small squeal. Yael decided to leave it open for her escape, then slowly pulled the curtains aside.

To her surprise, the small house was not one large open space; she entered a sparsely decorated bedroom and closed the curtains behind her. Allowing her eyes to adjust, she scanned the room and confirmed it was empty before making her way towards the door.

It was cracked just enough for her to see out into the living area. The man she was here to kill was sitting at a card table on the opposite side of the room. It would be easy to take him from here, but she wouldn't. Not until she saw his face. Not until she knew he was the right man.

Opening the door enough to slip through, she stepped out silently and aimed as she cleared the room. He was alone, totally absorbed in a *Jerry Springer* episode about threesomes and cheaters. Taking a few steps into the galley kitchen across from her, she knelt under the pass-through window and started her count.

One...

Two...

A sound from the bedroom startled her. Scrambling forward,

she crawled into the open space next to the counter, grateful the home lacked appliances.

When she heard the chair scraping against the living room linoleum, she knew the man had heard it too. Just as she peered around the cabinets to catch a glimpse, a tall figure came bounding out of the bedroom.

The man of the house spoke his last words.

"Mother fucker!"

Hearing the scuffle, she stared at the bedroom door knowing it was her only chance of escape. A horrible scream filled the house, then another.

Standing tall, her head hit the corner of the vent hood above her. Blinding pain told her she'd have a lump, but when her eyes met his, she felt nothing.

The man was still fighting for his life and didn't notice her. But Vitto did.

Sprinting out of the kitchen and reaching the bedroom in just three, wide strides, she heard the growl and felt him closing in. She slammed the door behind her and locked it, then ran to the window.

The bastard had closed it on his way in.

A loud thud sent her heart into her stomach, but she turned to see the door was still locked. Pulling the window ledge until her nails broke, she realized her mistake.

"Mother fucker!" Yael rasped, repeating the man's epithet with feeling.

Prying open the locks on either side of the window as she frantically watched the door, she slid the window up with ease and fell into the night.

Following her feet as fast as they would carry her, she ran into the darkness, kicking up dirt as she went. Sixty seconds later, she dove into her car and started the engine. The moment she left the street, she opened her phone and dialed Johhny.

"I need an appointment!"

"Kid, what the -"

"I need an appointment, Johhny!" Her voice cracked as she screamed again, "*I need a fucking appointment!*"

CHAPTER TWENTY

Johhny walked back into the office and handed Yael a roll of toilet paper.

"This is all we got, kiddo," he said apologetically.

"Thanks, Johhny."

The Don sat back in his chair and studied her, sliding his jaw back and forth. He hadn't said much as Yael explained her story, but Johhny had a lot of questions. Mainly…

"Who were you working for that night?"

Yael frowned. "I told you, I don't work for *anyone*."

"You work for us," Johhny offered.

She started to shake her head, then stopped. "Okay, you're right."

Johhny shot her a glare. "Am I missing something? As far as I know, you've picked up all your payments."

"Lay off, Johhny," the Don warned.

What the fuck? Johhny wondered. Eyeing his cousin warily, he found his seat to join them once again.

The one thing he never understood about this particular hire… was why the Don continued to give her so much leeway. What was so special about this girl that he believed she was trustworthy? How did they know she was for real?

For two years, Johhny was forced to investigate a mole within the ranks of the Family. When they discovered it had been Yaya all along, killing for free as some sort of vigilante, Johhny had his doubts. Though he liked her well enough, there was a bizarre mystery surrounding her methodology. The marks she chose, the jobs she declined — it all seemed so arbitrary.

If Yaya behaved more like the killer she was, he probably wouldn't notice her at all. But the girl acted like a sullen teenager half the time, and his cousin took it all in stride. Problem was, Sam didn't take anything in stride. It wasn't in his nature.

Tonight she showed up claiming that Vitto was following her and interrupting her work…yet, she didn't work for anyone else? That would make her a psychopath serial killer or a vigilante — and neither were welcome on any Family payroll. Yet here she was.

Not only did she kill for the Family, which was a bit of a grey area as far as he was concerned, but she was now running the bar? And tonight, she was getting a special meeting with the Don. It was rare anyone met with the Don directly — that's what Johhny was here for.

Every time he asked the Don who the girl was, he brushed him off like it wasn't *his job* to know. As the *consigliere* for the regional boss, he was required to know everything and everyone in this organization. As the girl's handler, he was required to keep tabs on her work and any activities that would affect the Family. So why the hell did Sam keep brushing him off? Nothing was adding up, yet he was expected to play it cool?

The Don's question interrupted his brooding. "So this is the second time he saw you?"

Yael shrugged, a look of dejection plastered on her face.

Johhny frowned, eyes darting back and forth suspiciously. "The second time?"

"It would have to be more, right? If he knew where I was already…he had to have followed me from the tunnels last week."

"And you're sure about that?"

Staring blankly at the Don, she nodded. "Deadly sure."

Johhny wasn't buying it. And he definitely didn't appreciate being treated like he wasn't in the room after being invited in.

Turning to the Don, Johhny asked, "You ever seen Vitto?"

To his surprise, he nodded. "Once."

"How'd you manage that — and live to tell?"

The Don glanced at him, then looked pointedly at Yael. "We'll talk."

Johhny gave him a look of his own. "Yeah, we will."

Clearing his throat, the Don closed his eyes and rubbed the bridge of his nose. "We're all gonna take a break," he said quietly. "Johhny, let Bruno know he's taking over The Lieu."

Yael sucked her teeth, but said nothing.

"And you," he continued, pointing his finger with a wag, "can you do your side work without drawing any more attention to yourself?"

She shrugged.

"What side work?"

The Don and Yael both looked at Johhny, then each other.

What the fuck? he wondered again.

Ignoring him, the Don sighed and walked around the desk to help Yael stand. Steering her towards the door, he gave her a warning.

"Young lady, you would do very well to watch your back. Vitto is a Peccati. Every generation of the Ybor Italians had a Peccati. As far as the Family is concerned, Vitto has the same divine protection as his fathers before him. I hope you can say the same."

Johnny watched as the Don pushed the door shut and steadied himself. "You alright there, Sam?"

"Huh?" The Don looked up as if he'd forgotten he wasn't alone. "Oh, yeah. Yeah, I'm good, Johhny."

"You mind telling me what's really going on?"

Shuffling towards his liquor cabinet, the Don shook his head. "Why do you always think there's a problem, Johhny?"

"You don't?"

"Back off, Johhny," the Don cautioned as he poured himself a tall glass of bourbon. "We got everything handled, didn't we? And you know how these guys can get about their territory…what, you've never seen two executioners go at it?"

"That kid ain't a executioner!"

"Exactly."

Johhny threw his hands up.

"Hey, what the hell is your problem, Johhny? Why don't you tell me what's really going on here?"

"Hey, I could ask you the same thing!"

The Don slammed his glass onto the desk. "Yeah? Well, I'm asking *you*! Here and now, what is it you want to bring to the table?"

Stammering, Johhny knew he'd been cornered. "You're a son of a bitch, you know that?"

"I guess it runs in the family, John Boy."

"Aw, fuck off, Sammy."

CHAPTER TWENTY-ONE

After hours of waiting for her to show her face, Ms. Peachy Keen finally walked out of the bar. Starting the car and watching her walk down the strip, Stacey waited to see where she would turn before driving down 7th Avenue. As she'd guessed, the girl was parked behind Margarita's.

"Hey, princess," she called out in a low voice.

Yael looked around in confusion.

Stacey pulled up and parked the car, blocking her in. "Yeah, bitch. It's me."

"Geez, Stacey! What the fuck do you want from me?"

Laughing bitterly, she obliged. "Everything." When she saw the younger woman roll her eyes, she snapped. "Bitch, I want the fucking money. I want what's owed to me!"

"I don't have your money," Yael said flatly.

Stacey's eyes flared. "Liar! O told me everything."

Yael gasped.

"Yeah, bitch. I know *all* about your little *contract*. I also know Xay had money everywhere, and according to O, you got the fancy lady's money, too. You're going to give it to me — one way or another."

"You're crazy."

"Oh, I'm crazy?" Stacey shook her head and leaned out the window, clinging to the door in her anger. "Bitch! Don't you know you were just another stupid hoe for him to turn out? Do you know how many girls we turned out together?"

"Stop it!"

"Nah, let's talk about it. I got time."

Yael looked around the lot and back at her car.

Stacey smiled at her conundrum. The naive little bitch was *scared shitless!* Enjoying the new sense of power, she decided to toy with her.

"You know, it was me who taught him how to love a woman. I was his first, his last, his everything. When his daddy bought the dojo and the house next-door, I thought that man was *so* fine! That is, until Xay had his first growth spurt. Mmm!

"I started him off real young, doing things I knew no other girl his age would do…and it worked. From the day I took his virginity, he was hooked on me. And you know why he liked me the best?"

Tears were falling down Yael's face as she stood rooted in place, staring at her feet.

Sizing her up, Stacey knew it was time to go for blood. She'd seen Peachey at the dojo and taken her for a fool. Even when confronted at Margarita's, the girl would freeze until someone saved her. Stacey was willing to bet she could make the girl crack in no time.

"I bet you never asked him for it. I bet you never *begged*. But me? I gave him everything he wanted, and then I asked for more. I showed him exactly how to make me hurt real good, 'cause I knew he needed it.

"And he knew I knew what was in them little *cocktails*. He also knew I didn't need any help. He could have me any way he desired. I bet you couldn't say the same, Ms. Peachy."

"You're sick."

"Oh, so you knew, too?" Stacey shrugged. "Well, the way I see it…Xay called me more in the last two years than he had since we were in our twenties. Even if you thought you were doing something, obviously, it wasn't enough. He still had plenty to spare for me. *Plenty*! So what were you really doin'?"

Yael's face turned to stone. "You're disgusting."

"Xay didn't seem to think so. Oh, I'm sorry. I meant to say '*sensei*'." She let out an ugly cackle, slapping the car door as she lifted her false lash at the corner of her eye.

"He's dead."

Stacey's eyes narrowed.

Yael drew herself up to her full height. "I'm glad he's gone. He was a horrible man."

Shaking her head, she laughed and then stopped short. "Only a weak ass female would say something like that. You don't deserve shit from him."

"Maybe you deserved him," Yael said quietly.

"Yeah, and I deserve my money, too! You don't seem to think his money was so horrible, or you woulda been paid up."

Yael looked around the lot again and shook her head. "You know what, fuck it. I got the money to fix my bumper. Do you have the money for a new car?"

Watching as the girl turned on her heel and opened her door, Stacey wondered if she was serious. When the car turned over and lurched into reverse, she sped off.

"That's okay, bitch!" she hollered out the window behind her. "I got somethin' for that ass!"

Barreling down 16th, she tried to cut down 6th but almost hit a pedestrian. By the time she made it around the block, Yael's car was gone.

"Fuck!"

She'd have to be more patient next time. Stacey knew the girl would never hand over the money willingly. It didn't matter, because she also knew just the goons to call. All she had to do was find out where the princess stayed...

Thinking about how many times Olivier asked about the little bitch, she punched her horn and let out a scream of frustration. The man was as bad as Xavier, just as lusty and far more temperamental. But he had helped her get over the initial shock of losing Xay, and now thanks to his near-constant chatter, she was one step closer to getting what was hers.

JANUARY

CHAPTER TWENTY-TWO

Yael yawned. A small, puffy cloud floated along slowly in the crisp breeze, appearing so close it seemed she could reach out and touch it.

Today was her first day off since Thanksgiving. She had been surprised it worked out so well, and was again later when Joe's schedule suddenly cleared up after closing a case. Though Monday would be a busy day and she would have to work the holiday, the next few days leading to her birthday were hers and hers alone.

Well, not exactly. But time spent with Joe was usually so peaceful she likened it to being by herself. And now that things had died down, she was happy to spend the weekend being recharged by his presence.

They were up at dawn, where Joe surprised her with a gift she never knew she needed. Both of their bedrooms had a wall of what she previously believed to be standard built-in shelving units. Today, Joe revealed that each layer of shelves actually formed a ladder, with the steps leading up to an area of the house he called 'the cockpit'. It was an apt name for the small crow's nests he'd built into the rooftops. The trap door looked like a standard attic door, but it opened straight up and led to a smooth, wooden bowl atop the house.

Yael smiled as a gust of wind swirled around her and tightened the plush velvet throw she'd carried up with her to enjoy the sunshine. When she and Joe climbed outside to watch the sunrise, he laughed when she asked him to build her one. To learn she had a space of her own right above her bedroom closet left her downright giddy.

She was excited to relax in her own cockpit tomorrow; Joe said they would be able to see each other from either roof. But she was exhausted after spending a beautiful morning laughing with him.

Maybe I will take that nap, she mused sleepily.

Joe was in bed just down the steps, having succumbed to the effects of the mimosas they'd consumed on the way back from their walk up Bayshore Boulevard. The trip would have been at least three hours, but after turning around at the Pirate Ship, he suggested they stop at the The Colonnade Restaurant for drinks and a seafood brunch.

Pushing off of the seat of pillows she made herself earlier, she opened the latch and pulled up the door until it locked in place. Once she checked that the coast was clear, she tossed the pillows and blanket through the opening and then climbed down.

She was happy to learn that Joe was handy around the house and just as creative as she was. The prospect of investing in real estate and flipping houses seemed more exciting if he'd be there, too.

Joe was still sound asleep on the bed, sprawled out on his back like a starfish. Thankful she'd already showered, Yael climbed into bed and curled up next to him with a contended sigh.

YAEL SHIFTED IN THE BED, an uncomfortable sensation bringing her to consciousness and forcing her eyes open. The curtains were drawn, but she gauged it to be late afternoon in the blue haze of her foggy vision. Something was digging into her hip. She reached to grab Joe's cell phone and toss it across the room, annoyed he'd brought it to bed on their day off. As her hand pressed against the offending bulge, she let out a soft gasp when it gave beneath her fingers and brought a loud groan from Joe.

Now I'll never get back to sleep.

Adrenaline flooded her system — or was it something else? She wasn't sure. But she did her best to squeeze her eyes shut and calm her breathing. One thing she wasn't about to do was embarrass herself *again*.

When her mind wouldn't cooperate and kept bringing her thoughts back to his hard dick springing out of his briefs, she switched to thinking about their morning together. Yet, romantic as it was, she swore she could feel his heartbeat pulsing on her leg.

Stop it, she scolded. Of course she was just being ridiculous.

But the longer she did her best not to move, the more stiff they both became. And soon, she was walking the tips of her fingers along her side until she felt him once again. Gripping the thick member through his shorts, she found she could move it up and down if she gripped it just right.

Joe caught her wrist and held it firm, and for a moment she felt the usual deflated sense of failure. But when he guided her hand up the leg of his basketball shorts and she felt the smooth hardness of his head, her excitement returned times ten.

Rolling onto his side, Joe clasped both of her cheeks and drove his tongue deep into her mouth. Wrapping her hand around his shaft, she pulled up and down slowly, intrigued by the new sensation. She did her best to focus on her work, but his onslaught did not make it easy.

When his hands roamed to pulled down the shorts she borrowed from him, Yael began to wonder what might be happening. It was Joe's middle finger rubbing her clit, then slipping inside her that made her realize she didn't care.

"Oh, wow," she cooed, closing her eyes to savor the feeling.

He slid in and out slowly, then buried his finger inside until her eyes rolled back into her head. She moaned as he leaned in closer and dug in deeper with every stroke.

Suddenly, he stopped. But she had no time to think, for just as suddenly he was pulling off her shirt, yanking down her shorts, then removing his own clothing. Seeing him like this — watching him gaze upon her nakedness with a ferocious hunger in his eyes — she found it hard to breathe.

Joe was absolute perfection from head to toe, an Adonis in rare form. The intensity in his eyes as he feasted on her in the shadows gave him a dark look, which somehow only improved his handsomeness.

Even here in the late afternoon haze, the golden tips of his shoulder length dreadlocks stood out against his sienna brown skin. His thick, muscular body was toned and cut in all the right places, but what she found most impressive was the raw, masculine energy emanating from his being. When her eyes landed on his powerful erection, the sleepy spell she was under began to fade as the panic set in.

She met his eyes again, confused by the maddening sense of need, the urgent craving to feel his touch, and the odd sense that she would ruin the moment if she moved a single muscle. When his full lips parted, revealing his straight white teeth, she wondered if he was trying to tell her something.

Joe shook his head and fell beside her onto the bed, causing her to let out a nervous giggle. Then he climbed on top of her, sliding his dick across her wetness and wedging himself between her thighs. Planting small kisses across her face, he began moving his hips into hers until his shaft rested along the length of her lips. Each time he ground into her, she could feel his hardness glide across her clit. She was in heaven.

He kissed her again, this time on the lips and with great hunger. She couldn't deny him, wrapping her arms around his neck as she bucked her hips up to receive him. They had simulated sex like this before, but the lack of clothes and the promise of more was a shock to her senses. Just as she was about to explode, Joe jumped back onto his knees with a growl.

Yael gasped, completely bewildered by his departure. Surely he didn't mean to tease her?

But he returned, this time to brace himself over her as he kissed her and rubbed his head up and down her lips. When the tip of his head thrust into her wetness, she squeezed her eyes shut, anticipating pain. Kissing her to distraction, Joe settled in above her and held himself steady.

It was strange; the only pressure she felt was from his lips and the rounded intruder at her entryway. He slowed his kisses, swirling his tongue around hers with a groan here and there, until he moved his lips to her neck. In spite of the nervous butterflies in her belly, her body was electrified, his kisses leaving her completely overwhelmed.

It was his lips wrapped around her nipple that did her in, immediately bringing her to orgasm and causing her hips to buck involuntarily. He penetrated deeper as he quickly kissed his way to her mouth, then fucked her with his tongue. When another orgasmic wave hit her, he dropped down onto the bed, driving himself deep into her tight wetness with full force.

The pain she expected did not come, and the discomfort she felt lasted only seconds. Joe pushed deeper and deeper, grinding his pelvis against her clit and kissing her until she melted, coming again and again.

"Joe," she moaned through his kisses, "I think I'm going to -"

Moments later, she came to, staring up at Joe as he watched her with a smug smile. She knew she would get him back one day, but for now...

"No more kissing," she breathed out. "I want to feel it all."

Letting out a primal growl, Joe pulled himself out until only the tip remained inside, then slammed all the way back in again, and again, and again, and again...

CHAPTER TWENTY-THREE

Yael gasped and plopped onto the cockpit bench, sprawling out with a laugh as she tried to catch her breath. Losing her virginity had taught her many things, but two important facts stood out to her. For one, sex was a great workout. And for two, she *loved* sex.

"I'll be right back," Joe said with a grin, leaning to kiss her heartily.

"More wine," she giggled, swatting at his behind as he climbed down into the house.

For almost two weeks now, she and Joe had sex every chance they could. This morning when his flight was delayed due to foul weather, she feigned ill and left work a half hour into her shift. They were still due for rain later in the evening, but they'd been up in the cockpit for hours.

It took a few days for her to find her rhythm, to learn how to move her body with such a large man so close…as well as inside. She almost lost hope — that is, until she discovered the power of *doggy style*. It was in this leveraged angle that she would find her sweet spot. Coincidentally, it was also the position that led Joe to unleash.

In ten days, they'd christened every room in the house, almost broken the dining room table, and given Yael rug burn. But it was in the last three days that she began bending over the moment they started…finding out very quickly that Joe loved to watch her throw her ass. And throw it she did.

Now it was a competition, and her sweet, kind, courteous man was determined to win. It was strange to admit, but after years of hearing about making love, Yael found it overrated. She enjoyed the moments where Joe tried to fight the urge to come by fucking her brains out, hoping she would give in before he did. Making love was like a cool down, and she much preferred the hard work of a good fuck.

The thought of Joe slamming into her a few minutes before made her walls quiver. Closing her eyes, she remembered how he reached around to rub her clit as he fucked her hard from behind. And that moment when he lifted her by her waist so he could put his tongue in her ear…

"Fuck," she moaned, wondering what was taking him so long. Tossing her head back, she decided she would strike a pose to prepare for his arrival.

It didn't take much for him to want her. And after months of keeping his hands mostly to himself, she was happy to find out he had such drive and endurance. At first he complained, though it was obvious he was teasing her; but after a few days, he simply stripped and jumped into action. His possessive, aggressive nature came out with the flip of this sensual switch; sometimes, she felt like she was fucking a lion in a man's body. Another shiver went through her as she recalled the deep, guttural sounds he would make in her ear or against her lips. Everything the man did drove her insane!

She hoped that one day soon, he'd be ready to try *other* things, but she didn't mind waiting. When Joe sat her down and explained that most people didn't have an orgasm from kissing, she had trouble believing him. But *both* of them had been shocked by their shared blessing these last few weeks.

Joe was oddly apologetic after their first time. He explained that he had some doubts about her virginity, but not anymore. She was only a little hurt. And in truth, ever since the sexual tension between them was broken, they had even fewer misunderstandings and miscommunications than before.

She watched as a bird dove straight down towards the water, pulling up after a hundred feet and flying back up towards the clouds. Another bird followed. Yael laughed as she watched the birds play in the pocket of air, feeling a lot like a bird herself.

Free as a bird, yeah yeah…

The Erykah Badu melody flowed in and out of her head as Joe came climbing up the ladder. Yael grinned, then drew her knees to her chest and spread her legs. Resting the fingers of one hand on her clit and sucking her index finger into her mouth, she met Joe's eyes as his head popped into the cockpit.

"Jessum peace," he moaned, eyes roaming from her bare breasts to her slick lips. "The Lord is my shepherd. I see what I want."

Yael bit her lip and winked.

CHAPTER TWENTY-FOUR

"Are we sure this is our guy?"

"I think so."

"I can't believe they didn't call us sooner!"

Joe looked at Weaver and shook his head. "Most of our vic's were Italian, this guy's Asian. The original request only asked for mob-related victims with the exsanguination signature. It might make for more work, but we'll need to broaden the parameters."

Weaver was on ten. "We're smack in the middle of the hot zone. This could be his neighbor — his neighborhood. How do we know this isn't an escalation?"

Joe shook his head again and called to Clancy. "Well, laddie? What you got?"

Poking his head out through the kitchen pass-through, Clancy asked, "Did anyone say why the neighbors waited so long to call it in?"

"They didn't call for this," Joe corrected. "He was behind on his rent in December. Landlord came by and thought things looked a bit off, but it wasn't until he questioned another tenant down the block that he called the cops."

Clancy raised a brow. "Why?"

"Neighbor said the victim appeared to have sold his appliances a few months back. Appliances came with the house, so the landlord tried to file a police report. Cops recognized the smell from the front door."

Joe, Clancy, and Weaver gathered in the only clean spot in the cramped living room and studied the bloody walls and furniture. When they were brought in on the case, the files indicated the cause of death to be dismemberment. It wasn't until they received the pictures and the autopsy results that they saw the similarities with their seemingly unsolvable case.

Weaver scanned the room. "So he stabs him, knocks him out, and saws him up while he's still breathing? Again, I have to ask — are we sure this is our guy?"

Clancy stepped away from the angry firecracker and pretended to study the bloody wall behind them.

Joe sighed. "Anything new from forensics?"

"All the blood came from the victim, if that's what you mean."

"What about this?" Joe asked, tracing his gloved fingers along a large dent in the wall next to the bedroom door.

Clancy perked up and leaned in. "Could have been a struggle?"

Weaver shook her head irritably. "This guy lived here for years. We don't know if that's new or came with the place."

Joe leaned in and looked at the cracks in the wall. "I think he's right, Weave."

Pointing at the blood splatter along the cracks, it was clear one of the spray patterns had been split in two due to the wall damage.

"Well, shit."

"Doesn't that nix our profile of a lone female?"

Joe's heart skipped a beat. "Hopefully."

Clancy gave him a curious look.

"Anything to narrow it down," he recovered quickly, stepping away to examine the bedroom.

He was hopeful, though. Ever since he and Yael had been physical, Joe felt closer to her than ever. He knew sex was not some remedy meant to solve relationship problems, but it had given them a deeper connection. The more he felt he could trust her, the more he recognized he was projecting.

Of course, he still had questions and he wasn't in complete denial. It was clear she was holding back, and he often sensed a dark side was hidden beneath her lovely exterior. She'd yet to explain the need and use of the guns and ammunition she favored, which was the only reason he had to suspect her anymore. Once he learned the truth about that, he would stop making spurious correlations between her and this case.

"This is bullshit, and you know it."

Joe turned to Weaver in the doorway and nodded, understanding her frustration. "They *should* have called us sooner."

"You think! Old and cold, that's what we got here."

Watching her stomp away, he couldn't help but feel her pain. The scene was well over a month old, and there were still a lot of missing pieces.

A knock on the window got his attention. He walked over and pulled it open. "Was this unlocked?"

The agent nodded. "And we just got another witness."

Joe leaned out the window and looked down, then ducked to step through onto the patchy grass outside.

"The next-door neighbor's son just told her that he heard a bunch of sounds outside last month, sometime before Christmas. She remembers, too, because he tried to sleep with her in the bed when he got scared. Her boyfriend was over so, she sent him back to his room."

"What did he hear?"

"Actually, it's what he saw." The agent pointed towards the clothes line. "He went to lay down for a minute, but he heard something. Looked out of his curtains to check it out. Said he saw a lady run by, then a man leaned out this window."

"A lady?" Joe blanched. "What did she look like? Which way was she running?"

The agent shrugged. "All he remembered was the man in the window."

"Was it our vic?"

"No, he said he was a big man with dark hair."

"Tall, fat, wide?"

The agent shrugged again. "I tried to get a description, but all he would say is the guy was big enough to fill in the whole window. He knew it wasn't his neighbor because of the hair — our vic was balding."

"Is the mother cooperative?"

"Enough."

Taking a deep breath, Joe continued. "Alright, see if he can remember anything else. And get Nathan in; maybe if the boy sees a sketch of a man with dark hair he'll be able to fill in the gaps."

"On it."

"Find out what you can about our lady of the night!"

The agent nodded and walked away.

Joe sighed. So much for hope.

CHAPTER TWENTY-FIVE

"Not now, damn it."

Yael squinted her eyes and slowed down, turning off Bayshore Boulevard to pull over on a side street. She was almost home, but she knew better than to push through a vision. They came in their own time, not hers.

Parking the car, she took a deep breath and closed her eyes, leaning back as the scene drew her in.

She saw a man — in a chair.

To her surprise — his throat was slit.

She shuddered, disappointed by the thought of having to use a knife again.

Then — she heard a sound.

Was it in her vision? Or was it coming from the real life street she was on?

Before she could figure it out, a blinding white light flashed before her.

She screamed in agony, wondering if she'd been hit by an oncoming car. But she couldn't move, couldn't open her eyes, couldn't see anything except the white light.

Gasping for air, Yael grabbed the steering wheel as soon as she came to.

"What the fuck?" she asked tearfully, wiping her eyes.

Sometimes her visions came easy. Sometimes they hurt like hell. She'd only had a few since they started, but she decided once and for all that she preferred the old way. A cryptic dream she pieced together like a puzzle was far more tolerable than this nonsense.

Yael did her best to collect herself, and after a few minutes of crying, the pain in her forehead began to subside. Though she was technically not on the payroll, she went with her gut and opened her phone to dial Johhny.

"Kid, I'm kinda busy here."

"Well, hello to you, too."

A long sigh escaped him. "How can I help you?"

Shifting in her seat, she pushed aside the urge to pout and continued. "Any chance you need some help in New Tampa?"

After a moment of silence, he answered. "How did you…you know what, never mind. When can you get out there?"

"Tonight?"

Johnny sipped his drink. "Negative, ghost rider. This one's gonna take some finesse. Meet me on top of the parking garage tomorrow afternoon."

"Which garage?"

"I think you know the one."

Yael's jaw dropped open as she heard the line disconnect. It'd been at least a month — maybe longer — since she'd seen him in person. She couldn't help but wonder what might have happened since then. Johhny wasn't exactly a nice guy, but she didn't know him as one to deliver such a low blow.

Maybe he's dealing with something?

Yeah, he's human, too.

An odd statement, but true. Yes he was just a man, but the way he operated in his general nonchalance could throw anyone off. There was something about Johhny that seemed robotic and artificial. She'd known him for almost a year and still knew nothing about him.

Seems to me he would prefer it that way, she sulked.

Less than ten minutes later, Yael walked through the door in a huff, still bothered by Johhny's comments. Swaying between guilt and irritation, she wondered if the Don was okay, or if something had happened at The Lieu? And what about the hit on the Don's life? Had that been resolved yet?

She sighed. The dull ache developing between her eyes said it was time to let it go.

What was it that Eileen always said?

"Not my circus…"

No, it wasn't. She didn't need to worry about the Family, for the Family could worry about itself.

She and Joe were finally building something special. She and Fred were beginning to make some headway learning the ins and outs of human trafficking. Fred and Joe were the only *family* she needed to worry about anymore.

Yael couldn't wait for Joe to return from his latest trip to DC. She stared out the window at his house, tearing up and wishing he could hold her now. She decided to take a shower and get some rest, though she wondered if she'd be able to sleep at all.

When she looked into the mirror to pull her hair from its confines, she was surprised to see the faint red kiss of lipstick on the bridge of her nose.

"What the -"

Only it wasn't on her face. She couldn't remember leaning over the counter to kiss the mirror, or the last time she wore red lipstick…

She took a step forward and went pale. It wasn't a kiss. And it wasn't lipstick.

Stumbling backward, Yael's stomach turned as she stared at the bloody fingerprint on the mirror — perfectly aligned with the center of her forehead.

CHAPTER TWENTY-SIX

Johhny threw a maroon polo shirt her way.

"Make sure you're wearing those when you get there. And don't forget the magnet. Those rent-a-cop guards got nothing better to do, you know?"

"Uniform, badge, car magnet. Got it."

Johhny paused and sized her up.

"What?"

Closing his trunk, he wiped the dust from his hands and crossed his arms as he leaned against the bumper. He lit a cigarette, watching her all the while. "You know, you still didn't tell me how you knew about this job…"

Swallowing her angst, Yael tried to think of a response. Her nerves were shot. "Why do I get the feeling we have a problem, Johnny?"

"No problem at all," he said coolly.

She shook her head and tried a different angle. "Why did you guys agree to let me in on it if there were questions?"

"There was no agreement. This guy's overdo. You called."

Squinting suspiciously, she tilted her head to ask, "So the Don?"

"He wants the job done."

Yael stared at him blankly as he gave a slight shrug, pulling another drag from his cigarette. Did she really need to ask? "Did you call Vitto?"

Johhny shook his head. "Vitto is no longer on our payroll, but that don't mean much. Watch your back, kid."

Flicking his cigarette to the ground, he turned on his heel and left.

———

YAEL WALKED to the edge of the garden to peek around a tall shrub. It was just after sunset and the streetlights were not yet lit, giving her the cover she needed to move from house to house.

When she arrived at the gate an hour ago, Johhny's plan went off without a hitch. The medical delivery company had called ahead to warn the guard about her arrival, and she'd made the delivery to an unsuspecting neighbor before parking her car at a dead end in the back of the subdivision.

Her mark lived in the very front of the neighborhood in the home centered at the main intersection. With nowhere to park her car, she decided it best to study a map of the streets while she waited and then go on foot. There really was no other choice; at least now she would know her getaway route ahead of time.

Unfortunately, her vision was once again blurred by anxiety and fear. To her credit, she had every right to be a mess. But fear was nothing new to her; she knew how to work with and around it to get the job done. This hit would be no different.

Last night gave her the reminder she needed. There was no one to call. No one would come to her rescue. But what she could do was watch her back and ensure she wasn't followed again. What she could do was focus on the light at the end of the tunnel. After all, it was the only tactic that ever worked before.

Joe would be home by the time she was finished. And she would be able to stay at his house for the rest of the week while she found her strength.

Just a little bit further.

Yes, just as as she remembered, the McMansion was right up ahead. Even though most of the backyards were the same in the cookie-cutter neighborhood, this one was the only one with a fence. Luckily, the trellis on the side of the house would get her in easily.

Unless…

No! No questions!

Since she could only make out bits and pieces of the house in her vision, she couldn't quite remember how she was supposed to get inside. Or for that matter, where she would find her mark. In such a big house, this could certainly be an issue. But she trusted the *knowing* would kick in.

Any minute now…

Climbing up the trellis, she stared into the pool area and listened for any sign of activity. The waterfall and fountains in the pool were loud, so she climbed the rest of the way and hoped they masked the sound of her arrival.

She landed with a soft crunch and quickly slid against the wall to search for security cameras. Finding none, she walked towards the open sliding doors and poked her head into the house. The smell of burnt olive oil and garlic overwhelmed her senses. A large living space was to her left and the kitchen was to the right. Thick columns and oversized art blocked her view beyond the living room, but all seemed quiet.

The same lights she saw on her initial drive past the house seemed to be on now, and she wondered if anyone was home this Saturday evening. Johnny told her the man had a family, but they were a busy bunch. She'd hate to have to come all the way back, but she hoped the open doors indicated someone was home.

Yael still didn't know what to expect, but she vaguely remembered stairs; she drew her gun and started up the steps in the corner of the kitchen. When she reached the top of the long hallway, she found the second floor to be eerily quiet.

Reminding herself that she'd checked for a tail numerous times on her way here, she shook off the terrible feeling that Vitto was waiting for her. She knew what happened when she ignored her dreams and visions — she had no intention of starting now.

Almost there, she assured herself.

But calming her nerves was not producing the intended outcome. She needed to know which of the many doors ahead of her would lead to a swift end. As long as she was freaking out, she was out of luck. Alas, the only thing she could hear was her own heartbeat.

A man in a chair flashed into her mind.

Yes!

Stepping forward with renewed vigor, she approached the first door and looked through the gap. The room obviously belonged to a young gamer; the setup looked like it was straight out of a catalog. But a little foot caught her attention and she stopped short.

"No," she whispered, surprising herself when she heard her voice.

Pushing away from the door, she crossed the hall and looked into the next room. Two little girls in dresses of sea foam green with ribbons flowing were holding each other, eyes squeezed shut tight. Blood soaked both their chests as they lay motionless in the thick silence.

Yael's eyes were wide with horror as she moved down the hall, her vision becoming clear. As she expected, a woman she believed to be the lady of the house was there in the next bedroom, shot in the back.

She knew she should run, as fast as she could, but something compelled her forward. Passing by several closed rooms, she recognized the door at the end of the hall and knew she had to open it.

Was this the scene of a true assassin?

Yael could *never* do such a vile thing — to kill an entire family for the sins of the father. Still, she had to be sure the job was done; why else would her vision bring her here?

The doorknob was cold, but it gave her a shock. Swallowing the gasp that nearly escaped her, she swung the door wide and aimed her gun inside.

Entering the master bedroom slowly, she stared at the man sitting upright in the chair at the foot of the bed. She crossed the room, stopping short when she saw the look on his face.

Shock. Terror. And to her dismay, he was dripping in fresh blood.

It was in that moment that the rest of Yael's vision came flooding in, activating something inside her she hoped she would never feel again. The creak from the closet door behind her left her paralyzed, but her mind was racing.

Was it all a setup?

Run, damn it!

What if it's just a kid?

But she knew — and felt — *his* presence. She knew the tension left in the air by his rage, his hatred for her. She *knew* that this was the end.

Her heart stopped when she heard the rustle of hangers.

Maybe it will be quick, she thought hollowly.

~~*How could you just give up?*~~

Run, damn it! Run!

But she couldn't move. Not that it would matter this time. He was never going to stop until —

The blip of a siren brought her to reality. Like the snap of a finger, she was released from the grip he had on her mind. The tip of his shoe caught her heel as she sprinted down the hallway, but she increased her stride. Jumping down the stairs and over the railing, she swung down and around into the kitchen and bolted out the sliding door.

The bloodcurdling scream of an infant called to her in the night. The sound tried to grip at her heart and pull her back, but she couldn't bring herself to stop. There was no trellis on the inside of the fence, and she had no time to find another exit. Running around the pool, she leapt onto a chair and reached for the fence.

Seconds later she rolled onto her side in the grass and scrambled to her feet to run towards the cover of darkness. When she looked back, no one followed.

Was Vitto so sick and twisted that he would stay to finish the job? Or was he already on the way to *her* house? She choked back a sob as she moved quickly though another backyard, praying the baby survived the night.

CHAPTER TWENTY-SEVEN

"They left the baby."

"Who's got access to the surveillance?" Joe snapped.

Clancy shook his head. "The guards say their system has been out for two weeks and the system in the house was turned off manually just after six."

"We almost had him!"

Clancy put his hand on Joe's shoulder. "This is the freshest scene we've had to work with, boss. We're closing in on him. In a way, this is a victory."

"How many bodies?"

"Five."

"You call that a victory, Clancy?" Brushing him off and walking down the sidewalk, Joe took a few deep breaths and tried to focus.

It was happening again.

Following the untimely death of his wife and son, he noticed he was losing his cool in the final moments of his cases. The therapist assigned by the Bureau last year was convinced he had developed a complex, but Joe felt that the diagnosis was a self-fulfilling prophecy. Yes, they died just as he was closing a big case. Why did that mean he should expect to relive the trauma towards the end of every future assignment?

Admittedly, this scene felt closer to home. A mother and her children, killed in cold blood? Yes… He was wise enough to know he'd arrived at the mental barrier once again, but it didn't make it any easier to get through. In fact, it was exactly this sense of overwhelming dread and doom that got him placed on leave. According to the therapist, it was his response to the feeling, not the feeling itself, that rendered him unfit for duty.

Not this time, he thought boldly.

No. This time would be different. This would be his breakthrough case, and from now on, he would be back to his old self. Taking a moment to think of what his old self would do, he turned to face the house and recap what he'd learned since they landed.

"Weaver," he called out. "Come here."

Jogging over, she stood before him and waited, a curious look on her face.

"A criminal on our watchlist happens to live in a neighborhood where a man down the street gets medical deliveries."

"There's the opening."

Joe nodded and continued. "The guards have been having issues with their system for weeks."

"*And* the delivery is usually only made once a week," she replied, scribbling furiously onto a notepad. "So we're checking the security company, the delivery company — and while we're at it, we're gonna need surveillance from pretty much everybody."

"How could we have gotten here faster?"

Weaver stopped writing and stared at him. "Land the plane on Bruce B. Downs?"

Joe sighed. "What made the guard call it in?"

She flipped back a page and skimmed it before reporting. "He *was* expecting a second delivery, but when the third guy came in he got suspicious. Called the delivery company but the switchboard was busy, which he said was unusual because they have a 24-hour dispatch he's spoken to before. Neither came back through the gate in time, so he called it in."

"If you hadn't of built that watchlist -"

He stopped short, turning towards the intersection.

"What?"

He blinked. "You said they never left?"

Weaver shook her head. "A little confusion there. Shift change — no surveillance."

"Jessum peace."

Clearing her throat, she gave him a salute and ran back to the house.

One hour, he thought miserably.

If they had arrived only an hour earlier, they might have been able to stop the next killing. Two hours earlier and they could have prevented these. Shaking his head, he unlocked the SUV and reached for a bag of gloves. When he saw the car approaching, his heart sank.

He missed Yael, more than he usually did.

But as quickly as the thought came and went, the familiar headlights brought a deeper sense of foreboding to his spirit. Holding up a hand to stop the driver, he stared at the dark tint on the window and tried to steady his breath.

"I thought that was you!"

"What are you doing here?" he gritted out, his stomach in knots.

Yael swallowed and licked her lips. "My boss needed a favor. You okay?"

Joe heard the nasally pitch of her response and knew she'd been crying. Casting a nervous glance at the house, he asked again, this time with more force.

"Yael, what are you *doing* here?"

"Well, I wasn't following you, if that's what you think!"

No, that wasn't what he thought at all. He looked over his shoulder at the chaos behind him.

"I'm sorry," she gasped. "You're working!"

Nodding absentmindedly, he stared past her to the rumpled shirt on the passenger seat. It was too dark to see anything else, but he wondered…

"Coming home soon?"

Joe took a step back and opened his phone, turning on the flashlight. "I'm not sure," he said, trying to appear calm as he shined the light onto the side of her door.

Yael shielded her eyes, looking past him to observe the commotion. "I thought you said it was all interviews and bureaucracy?"

Joe scratched the back of his neck. "Maybe a bit more than that."

"Oh," she replied, lowering her voice, "See you later?"

He gave her a blank look and turned toward the house. Catching a glimpse of Weaver as she went inside, he cleared his throat. "See you later."

Patting the roof and stepping back, Joe watched her drive away slowly. Using the light on his phone, he flashed it twice to signal to the officer at the corner to let her through the barricade.

The only way in or out of the neighborhood was the front gate. He looked down the street and sighed, turning the light off and flipping his phone shut. If he didn't do this now, he would never stop thinking about it. He walked back to the SUV and started it, driving the way she came. And, as expected, the road ended at a wide, empty cul-de-sac.

"*Bumbo*," he murmured.

For months, he did his best to trust her. He beat himself up for thinking of her every time the team attempted to reconfigure their profile. But when it came down to it, he just let a prime suspect walk away without saying a word. He broke protocol for this woman time and time again.

"What am I doing?" he wondered aloud, stroking his beard. "I *know* she's lying to me."

He sat and allowed his mind to wander, picturing the rectangular outline of dust on her driver door. Didn't he always tell her she should wash her car more frequently?

She lied to me, he thought again, the sadness sinking in deeper. It couldn't be the first time.

Heading back toward the crime scene, he decided to take a second look. Maybe he would have better luck this time around, now that he was fairly certain *his woman* was the one doing the damage.

CHAPTER TWENTY-EIGHT

Yael waved to everyone at the bar and gave them the best fake smile she could manage. All she had to do now was drop the deposit in the safe, and she would be home free.

The last couple of weeks had been lonely and filled with sleepless nights. Joe's work schedule picked up dramatically after their run-in at the crime scene, though she was beginning to wonder if that was really the case. He seemed distant and moody, and at times, completely uninterested. If she didn't know any better, she would think he was onto her...

Would that really be so bad?

Yes, it would be — but that didn't stop Yael from thinking about coming clean. She was so on edge and she hated lying to him, especially knowing it was his job to put people like her away. Deep down, she knew the only other option be to break things off, and she couldn't bring herself to even consider it.

No, she wasn't going down this track again. Once she got on that train of thought, it was difficult to get off. Besides, she knew Joe well. He was a straight arrow; if he had any idea what she was up to that night, she would have been locked up by now.

Enough!

She had to stop the spiraling. Yael tried to tell herself she was stronger, better than she used to be. She tried to distract herself with other things until she could convince herself things were going to be fine. It rarely worked, but she did try.

Vitto was once again a silent threat. Some days, she wished he would give up and go back to his miserable life. Other days, she told herself he already had. Knowing she wouldn't feel comfortable working with the Family until he was dead and gone made her sad for reasons she still didn't understand. Then again, what was one more reason to be sad when there were so many to choose from?

Without a plan for Vitto, Yael looked to Fred's efforts for encouragement. She wasn't really sure what he was building, but it looked intense. Of course, she should have made more progress on her own by now. Her excuses about not having the time were starting to wear thin. She was often too depressed to do anything other than work, and she didn't like having to explain herself to her cousin. They barely saw each other anymore, and she would need to rectify that sooner than later.

How about tonight?

Yes, tonight would be a good night to head to the Port and then stop by to see Fred and Tres. She had driven by in the last several months but it was time to take things seriously. Staring at the ships wouldn't save anyone's life.

What else am I supposed to do?

She didn't have a clue. It was weighing heavily on her mood, which made the days drag on. All she wanted was to be left alone, but the more she regressed into her old silence, the more unwanted attention she received. If one more person told her to smile, she'd

—

"We've got to stop meeting like this!"

Shooting daggers his way, she snapped, "We've got to stop meeting at all!"

Olivier made a face.

Turning around to try the other door, Yael searched the bar for Dallas and Bear. Cocking her head towards Olivier, she went out into the patio area and stalked towards the second exit. But he ran ahead of her and blocked her once again.

"Just listen to me, woman," he said in vexation. "It has been months since I made my offer, and I've done my best to wait for you. I won't be able to stay much longer. You do understand?"

"Are you fucking kidding me, dude?"

"No, I'm not," Olivier replied, his voice calm and soothing. "Whenever you're ready, I know we can work out a favorable arrangement."

"We both know you're in it for the money. Get lost, fuckface."

"You're hurt, I know."

"Look -"

"Let me finish!" His eyes were focused on something behind her, but he spoke with conviction when he said, "Marry me and you'll never have to work again!"

"Boss, you alright over here?"

Yael stepped around Olivier and walked towards the door. "Get a photo," she tossed over her shoulder. "He's banned, for good."

"Why, I don't think —"

She saw the flash of light and almost laughed, but when she heard Eileen and Jeanne loudly join the conversation, she chuckled in spite of herself.

FEBRUARY

CHAPTER TWENTY-NINE

F rederico cracked the front door and made a face. When he saw the woman standing on his porch, his eyes narrowed.

It'd been months since he had a visitor. Taking care of a kindergartner was a full-time job, leaving him very little time to focus on his tech company and the database for Yaya. He had just finished setting up a code to scan pornography videos for signs of abuse and trafficking and needed to test it out. As curious as he was to see her here, he really didn't have the time for bullshit.

"Whatchu want?"

Amber gave him a hurt look. "You ain't gon' open the door, Fred?"

"Hell nawl!"

She laughed. "Don't I know it."

He sucked his teeth. "I'm working. Ain't nothin' here for you."

"I wouldn't say all that."

Frederico looked at the suggestive wiggle she gave him and sucked his teeth again. "What 'bout yo' best friend?"

Amber had been friends with his ex for years, but that never stopped her from giving Fred the eye from time to time. She wasn't a bad looking girl, but she was well known around the neighborhood. Either way, no amount of hood goodness was worth the drama from his baby momma.

She shook her head and looked out towards the street, catching him by surprise. "She tryna join us."

Frederico slammed his door shut.

"Come on, Fred!" Laughing from the other side, Amber knocked and tried again. "I finally turned her out last night…"

Unlocking all the locks as Amber cracked up, he opened the door all the way and looked outside. There was no one on the main road, but…

"Whatchu mean?"

Reaching for his basketball shorts, she gave the drawstring a tug and smiled up at him. "I put her to sleep, Fred. And I can do it again."

Frederico shook his head. "Fuck her!"

Serafina was nothing but trouble — a fact they both knew. When he received custody of Tres, the county agreed to set up a restraining order against her due to her erratic behaviors. Why would she risk it? This had to be a part of a plot to destroy him, right?

Amber gripped his forearm and slid her fingers down in a sensual caress. "You must not be listening?"

"What -"

"She been bragging about that dick for the longest," she let out in exasperation. "And she been talkin' about gettin' some more — so much that she got herself *all worked up*."

She pulled him closer, speaking in a low tone. "So this morning, *we* decided to come get some dick."

"We?"

"Mhm," she said even lower. "And the way I see it, all we gotta do is put her to sleep…and then me and you can finally have some fun."

Frederico cocked his head to the side, mouth agape. It had been months since the last time he got any. Plus, Serafina had been quiet and on her best behavior for months. Had she finally changed?

Yeah, right!

But…maybe?

Stuck between a rock and a hard place, he wondered if he should beat off before he considered this offer?

Amber gave him no time to think. "I bet with your help, we can have her knocked out in no time."

"And she agreed to it?"

Brows lifting with a small smile, she said, "It was *her* idea."

Two redbones!

Frederico shook his head, trying to push the song from his mind.

"I been wanting this dick for a long time," she moaned out as she wrapped her hand around his growing hardness.

Two redbones!

Exhaling sharply, Frederico reminded himself that the song in his mind didn't even make sense. His ex was Italian — and Amber was a nice honey brown. Very nice…

Wait! Hell nawl!

"I don't got nothing for y'all," he said firmly. "This ain't the trap no mo'."

Amber stroked his dick, never dropping her eyes. "I'm here for something different, boy."

Girl, don't stop, keep going and relax me…

"Call her," he said huskily, doing his best not to get too excited as he forced the Boosie song from his mind.

She released him and walked to the edge of the porch, leaning over to wave and whistle. Then, sauntering his way, she squeezed past him in the doorway and gave him a wink.

"Let's get started," she whispered, running her fingers along the elastic of his shorts.

Following her into the house, Frederico let her slide his shorts over his hips. Dropping to her knees in front of him, she kissed his head and moaned, then popped it into her warm, wet mouth. Eyes darting between her and the door, his heart jumped when it swung open.

"Damn, y'all couldn't wait for me?"

The sound of her shrill voice made him soften slightly, his nerves getting the best of him as he contemplated the injunction in place. But Amber was obviously serious about getting what she wanted.

"Girl, stop," she said as she slapped his head against her cheek. "I told you he wouldn't believe we was for real. Close the do' and come get you some dick!"

Smirking at them both, Serafina shut the door and locked up. Frederico's stomach turned when he saw her strip down from the corner of his eye.

"Where the liquor at?"

Blinking, Frederico did his best to ignore her as she approached and dropped into place next to her friend. But it didn't take long for his eyes to fall on his mother's child.

Serafina pushed Amber's head down towards his balls and took over sucking his dick. Once she had shoved him all the way in to the back of her throat, she stared up at him with her green eyes wide open and waited.

Staring back at her, he recognized the dilation of her pupils and knew she was already high. Knowing her, it was Molly with an Irish coffee chaser.

But he didn't care.

Not today.

SERAFINA MOANED as Frederico pumped in and out, biting his lip as he felt Amber's tongue slide back and forth between them. Since their arrival two hours before, he and Amber had worked Serafina into her current stupor. Now, Amber was sucking her clit and licking his shaft, still fully clothed. He marveled at her focus.

"Give me that nut," she growled, angling her head to lick Serafina's clit furiously. Reaching up to palm one breast, she squeezed her hard pink nipple between her fingers and moaned into her pussy.

Seconds later, Serafina was bucking on his dick and pressing her best friend's face into her mound like nothing else mattered. Watching intently, he did his best not to lose himself in the feeling and maintained his stroke.

"Stop," she begged, gasping for air.

Frederico jumped back, pulling out as he held the condom in place. But Amber ignored her plea, instead lowering her head to shove her tongue into Serafina's pussy. Mouth open in shock, he watched with fascination while she bucked and screamed as Amber kept a finger pressed onto her clit.

"Damn," he breathed.

Amber lifted her head and lapped away, slowly returning to her clit and sucking it softly.

"Give it to me."

His ex was in her own world, eyes squeezed shut as she arched her back and rubbed herself against her friend's lips and tongue. As much as he couldn't stand the woman, he had to admit the scene before him was incredibly erotic.

She's no Mystique.

Frederico frowned and shoved the thought from his mind. Taking the condom off and tossing it onto the floor, he sat on the arm of his sofa and jacked off as Amber continued her task. Her mouth had been working nonstop for so long, he had to wonder if she'd have any strength left for him.

Kissing and licking her way up to Serafina's breasts, then her lips, she slipped a hand down to rub circles around her clit and shoved two fingers inside.

"Wake up," she barked. Then, kissing her deeply, she tried again. "Fi? Fina?"

Taking her hand from Serafina's thighs, she sucked her fingers clean as she watched him stroke. Then, she started to strip, a wide grin set on her face.

"I knew I'd have you one day," she whispered, walking around the couch toward the hallway. "Let's take a shower so we can start fresh."

Frederico scrutinized her naked form as she moved lithely down the hall, only somewhat shocked by her admission. Staring down at his baby momma, naked, snoring and fully sated, he shook his head and jumped to his feet. But when he heard the water start, a flash of blue paint flowing down the drain caused his step to falter.

Determined not to let the visions of a ghost ruin his fun, he marched into the bathroom with a new determination to fuck the dog shit out of the woman who just worked so hard to earn it.

CHAPTER THIRTY

The Department of Children and Families was located in Central Tampa in a neighborhood far outside Serafina's comfort zone. She hated coming here.

When she was young, the building was home to the Floriland Flea Market. Taken over by various state organizations and a few private companies, the building also housed the unemployment office, Medicaid, and the food stamp department. Each office was old and damp, having poor ventilation that was never updated, giving the spaces a filthy, dingy feeling. Fluorescents shone down to provide a sterile ambiance, the white spotlights bringing her attention to how nasty the place really was.

Though she never knew wealth, Serafina was born into a family with a rich legacy. Her childhood home in Ybor City was surrounded by dilapidated houses and dirty lots, but her mother Silvia raised them to be a proud people. Though the DCF offices looked and felt a lot like home, she refused to see it that way. The people that came here were beneath her. No court order was going to determine her future — or what she did in the meantime.

"Ms. Rizzoli?"

Serafina stood and followed her case worker down the hall into the cramped meeting room. The woman stopped to usher her inside, studying Serafina as she jotted down a note on a sticky pad.

Ms. Jackson was a short, stout, no-nonsense woman; Serafina hated her. And it wasn't because she was black — it was because she followed the rules. Everything had to be by the book with Ms. Jackson, and Serafina had grown accustomed to getting her way without much fuss. But if a fuss was what she needed…

"You alright?" she asked, a look of concern on her face as she slowly entered the room.

Dropping her chin, Serafina shrugged. "I'm okay, Ms. Jackson."

"Have a seat here," she said, still eyeing her suspiciously. "I'm glad we could finally talk. You know it's been months since you were issued this case plan and you haven't even started."

Serafina looked at the wall and shrugged. "I been trying…"

Ms. Jackson patted her hand. "I know, I know."

Flipping through her file, she made a few notes. Then, pulling out a form, she placed it on the table and pointed to the date with her pen.

"You know your drug test is tomorrow?"

Serafina nodded.

"Okay, um, you know what happens if you don't pass it, right?"

Serafina gazed at the woman, tears falling down her cheeks.

Ms. Jackson patted her hand again, then clasped it gently. "Why don't you tell me the truth? Are you high right now, Ms. Rizzoli?"

Closing her eyes, she nodded.

"I guess that explains why we've been avoiding rehab?"

Serafina bit at her cuticles.

Ms. Jackson sighed and made another note. "How long have you been using?"

"Just since yesterday," she lied.

"And what happened yesterday?"

Serafina sniffed. "I saw my baby daddy."

"Oh?" Ms. Jackson rechecked the file. "You two have an injunction here. You aren't supposed to be near him. How'd that happen?"

Serafina shook her head woefully. "I don't remember."

"You don't remember…what?"

Staring into the woman's eyes, she whispered, "Anything."

Ms. Jackson leaned forward in alarm. "What happened, child?"

"I don't know," she mewled pathetically, covering her face with both hands.

"Well, where was your son?"

"I don't know!" she snapped. "And he don't know either. He never sees him!"

"I don't understand?" Ms. Jackson flicked through the pages of her file. "Everything here says that your dependency case was going as expected: dad and son have a schedule worked out; he's been getting to school on time and his attendance is perfect; and dad says he's having fewer nightmares lately. What happened?"

"Y'all believed him? He's the neighborhood dope man!"

"I -" Ms. Jackson stopped short. "Why wasn't that mentioned before? He was cleared for placement?"

Serafina wailed. "Y'all took my son from me for nothing, and now y'all let him drug me and rape me! Y'all stole my son and gave him to a predator!"

"We - I -"

"I thought you said you were gonna help me get my son!"

Ms. Jackson stood and came around the table, trying to console her. "We're going to get everything handled, you just let it out."

Handing her a tissue and leaving the box in front of her, she ran to the door to flag someone down.

"Call the police!" she said in a harsh whisper.

Swiftly returning to her seat, she opened the case file and scanned the pages. Looking at her watch, she picked up her cell phone and dialed out.

"Hi, Mr. Moon? This is Ms. Jackson," she paused, impatience showing on her features. "Yes, I'm fine. I've got Ms. Rizzoli here and I just need you to confirm some things for me? Okay, great. Uh, how are things going with dad?"

Serafina listened as she stared at the table, fingers fidgeting in her lap.

"Oh, I see? And who is that?" Ms. Jackson scribbled another note. "So, about how often do you see him, then? Really?"

Doing her best not to smile, Serafina hid her face in her hands.

"Well, thank you Mr. Moon. There's likely going to be a change of placement here, so I'll be in touch. No, thank you!"

Ms. Jackson wrote another note and then stood to walk to the door, wringing her hands.

"What did he say?"

Turning to face Serafina, the older woman took a deep breath and explained. "The instructor said there's a woman who always takes your son home. Supposedly, dad hasn't been at more than a handful of events. He mentioned a tournament and some other special family night. That's it."

"I told you," Serafina spat out. "I told you the first day in court, but y'all didn't wanna listen. You don't even know where my son is, do you?"

Ms. Jackson shook her head. "He went home with the lady again, but hopefully he's safe and sound with dad for now."

"Now what?"

"Well, we've got a lot to do in a little time. Emergency placements can be challenging, to say the least. Obviously, he can't stay with dad, so it looks like he'll be with maternal grandma — oh, your mom. And you're in no condition to take your drug test — but we can delay that easily by getting you into a rehab facility tonight.

"For now, though, we need to deal with what happened to you yesterday. I have to ask, are you comfortable reporting this?"

Serafina nodded. "Absolutely. Fred won't get away with hurting me ever again."

"Okay. Give me a few minutes."

When she disappeared and closed the door, Serafina couldn't help but chuckle. This had worked out better than she could have planned.

MARCH

CHAPTER THIRTY-ONE

No bond?

Yael was still in shock. Six months ago when he received custody, she was thrilled that Frederico had been granted his one and only wish. He had his son and could raise him as he saw fit, and his crazy baby momma was legally required to leave him alone. Clearly, she had no idea just how bad things really were.

It'd been a week since he called her from jail, letting her know where to find his keys so she could go lock up the house. Due to the nature of his charges, and the fact that he had been given temporary custody of a ward of the state, he couldn't bond out. And worst of all, Serafina had falsely accused him of rape.

Well, was that really the worst part?

After hearing how he'd been treated by the judge, the case managers, the police, and even his own court-appointed lawyer the last six months, she was worried. Somehow, Serafina Rizzoli had gotten her child taken away due to neglect — and also convinced an entire courtroom that Frederico was capable of far worse. Every court session, he was spoken to like a criminal. Every check-in with the case manager, he was talked down to as if he didn't know that his son needed to be fed, clothed, and loved.

If Yael had known he needed her help, she would have been around more.

Yes, she knew that her nephew had been trained to call his own father a *nigger*. Yes, she understood that Serafina had been manipulating and brainwashing Tres for years. But...Fred was still his *father*. She thought the anger and rage coming from such a small body was only temporary — induced by the stress of all he faced.

She had no clue about anything.

How could she have missed so much? How could she have missed that Fred spent the last six months being dragged down by every single person he came in contact with?

Now she couldn't even *see* her nephew. All the hard work that had been done to help him forgive his father was likely undone when Tres watched Frederico's violent arrest last week. And from what Fred told her, Serafina's mother Silvia was even worse than her daughter — after all, she raised her. Hearing Fred break down knowing what his son would endure...it had taken everything out of her.

What if he never got out?

Or what if Vitto took *her* out while Fred was locked up?

They'd been making a lot of headway with their efforts to uncover possible signs of trafficking, but without Fred's focus, the only thing she could think about was avoiding Vitto.

A car honked behind her. Yael took a deep breath, realizing she was barely breathing. She glanced up absentmindedly at the green light, then hopped her foot to the gas pedal and crossed the intersection. Autopilot brought her this far, but the thought of Vitto led to thoughts of Joe...and thoughts of Joe...

She pushed him from her mind.

She and Joe had hardly spoken in the weeks that passed since they ran into each other at the crime scene. And the more she thought about it, the more she wondered about Vitto. What if he was planning a fate worse than death, just for her?

No.

She'd promised herself she wouldn't do this anymore. No more spiraling, no more planning a future filled with unhappy *what ifs*. No more. Spending this much time in her own fucked up head was probably how she could go months without noticing her cousin spiraling into depression. And if she could miss the obvious clues with someone she knew almost as well as she knew herself, there was no telling what she was missing in Joe's life.

You're doing it again! Right now!

Shaking her head, she tried her best to focus on the road. Less than a minute later, a blinding light came flooding in.

You've got to be kidding me, she whined, slowing the car so she could pull off Bayshore Boulevard before the vision took over.

The sound of honking brought her mind to focus. Another beat passed and she understood it wasn't a vision at all. Was she driving too slow? Checking her speedometer, she knew that couldn't be it. Even after slowing down, she was still over the limit.

What the hell?

The car behind her sped up and came close to hitting her, the blinding lights disappearing under the rear window.

"Hey!"

There was no one else on the road with them. Yael sped up and tried to get over, wondering why the driver didn't just go around. But when she swerved into the left lane, the car behind her did the same.

"What the *fuck*?"

Her adrenaline surged. She tried her best not to give in to the grisly images in her mind, but it was no use. The car was getting closer and closer, and she had to assume there was an endgame.

Speeding down the road, Yael did all she could to maintain control and keep her eyes on her two-ton assailant. Bayshore was a long, winding boulevard filled with curves and crosswalks. When she saw her speed clock in at over seventy miles per hour, she wondered if their aim was to force her to crash.

Watch the road, watch the road. Eyes straight!

Slowing to take a sharp turn, panic set in as the driver swerved alongside her, then attempt to ram her. Yael gasped. Cutting the wheel to avoid the impact, she floored it and moved past them again.

He's going to kill me.

There was no use denying it. It was inescapable. Vitto was no longer on standby.

Her father taught her how to drive in a Chevy Avalanche, and through the years she had learned a thing or two about getting the fuck out of dodge. But how was she supposed to fight fire with fire and not kill herself in the process?

How was she supposed to survive this one?

Yael slammed on the brakes. About a hundred feet ahead, the other car stopped, too.

"Why did I think that would work?" she cried.

Shifting into sport mode, she pressed the gas pedal to the floor again and zoomed forward, narrowly missing the bumper of the other car as they tried to cut her off. Bayshore would end soon, and there was a red light ahead that was almost never green. Checking the rearview, she wondered if she could successfully navigate a turn down a side street doing sixty miles an hour.

Wishing she'd grabbed her gun when she stopped the car, she

tried to reach for the glove compartment. Taking the quick little turns without two hands on the wheel was nearly impossible.

"Fuck, fuck, fuck!"

Vitto was gaining on her again, and they'd just run a red light, barely avoiding an accident. With only a mile or two left before another worst case scenario occurred, she had to figure something out. The only thing she could think to do was to turn around somehow; maybe more road would give her the idea she was searching for. Just as she thought to look for a way to trick him again, she saw the flicker of a reflector on the opposite side of the street up ahead.

No!

She couldn't help herself. Taking her foot from the gas pedal, she strained her neck, trying to see if someone was crossing the road. Vitto took the opportunity and fell in beside her, swerving sharply to hit her.

"Fuck!"

Leaning onto the horn as she held the wheel steady, she sped up and avoided another swerve. There *was* someone in the road — a woman — and she was pushing a stroller!

Yael yanked the wheel left, this time attempting to do some ramming of her own. Vitto cut left, then quickly right, trying to avoid a construction sign on the corner. Knowing she had little choice, she was forced to swerve into him again, narrowly missing the woman's heel.

The blinding light was gone; Vitto was no longer following her. For a few hundred feet, she continued down the boulevard in shock, the sudden silence weighing on her as she caught her breath. But a minute later, she was turning around and reaching for her gun in the glove box.

Creeping along, Yael noticed the stroller on the corner. Where had the woman gone?

Vitto!

Pulling closer to park in the turn lane, she exhaled sharply when she found the woman examining the wreckage.

"Are you okay?"

The woman turned to face her. "Oh! It's you!"

Yael stared at the car and asked, "Is he…"

"He?"

Frowning in alarm, Yael stepped out and tucked her gun into her jeans. She approached slowly, fearful that the woman might be a part of this, too.

"Oh!" She stared at the mess she'd made.

The digital construction sign was largely unharmed. The car that was chasing her was split down the middle on the driver's side. The flat base of the large sign was embedded in the hood. And there in the backseat…was Stacey's decapitated head.

"You saved me," the woman whispered. Glancing at the stroller across the street, she continued. "You saved us!"

Saved? Yael shook her head. She'd just killed a woman in cold blood — had a gun ready to finish the job. She was no savior.

The woman reached her hand forward, then stopped and asked, "Are *you* okay?"

She caught the sob as it slammed against her throat, pursing her lips against the pressure, denying it an escape from the turmoil within. Thick tears welled up in her eyes.

"Go."

Blinking, she tilted her head in question. The woman's face paled as she looked around, then up at the trees, and then nodded towards Yael's idling car.

"It's okay," the woman whispered. "Just go."

Yael stared at her.

The woman pulled her phone out of her pocket and dialed three numbers. "Hello, 9-1-1? I'd like to report an accident. The lady tried to avoid me, but…she's gone."

Giving her a small smile, the woman crossed the street at the sound of her crying child and didn't look back.

CHAPTER THIRTY-TWO

"Who the fuck gave you that authority, huh?"

"You did!"

"The hell I did, Johhny!"

"The job got done, didn't it?"

The Don exploded. "Are you fucking kidding me, Johhny? That was overkill and you know it. *She* didn't do that — so who the fuck did?"

"I think we both know the answer to that one, boss."

The Don threw his glass across the room before pointing at his cousin. "You're damn right, Johhny. You know I'm starting to wonder — what side are you on here?"

"Oh, you're kidding *me* now!"

The Don shook his fist. "You ask too many questions, but you couldn't handle the answers, Johhny! I can promise you that."

Johhny's eyes narrowed. "You see, this is exactly what I'm talking about, Sam. You and me? Never had a single fucking problem — not even over a woman. Nothin'! Now? Every time the kid's name is brought up, you're keeping things from me. What did you expect?"

"I have a right to privacy, Johhny!" the Don blustered, his face cherry red.

"Not where the Family's concerned."

The Don threw his hands up and swore in Italian.

"I say we go back to the way things were. Give the kid her old jobs back. The bar ain't the same without her and you know it."

"Oh please, Johhny," the Don groaned. "Now you're on *her* side? Fucking bullshit!"

Johhny shook his head. "I don't trust her and I don't know why you do. Either way, I can't keep an eye on her from here."

"Why won't you just drop it, Johhny?"

"*Because.* I am your *consigliere*. I am your cousin. I am your best friend. But when it comes to Yaya, I am in the dark — in more ways than one. How many times do I have to remind you — *this is my job*."

"I was in the dark when you sent her to do a job that wasn't even hers…"

"I told you — *she* called *me*. You still don't see anything wrong with that?"

Crossing his arms defensively, the Don shrugged. "I'd think you would say she was just doing her job, no?"

Johhny scowled. "Don't play stupid, Sam."

"Stop trying to get her killed, Johhny."

"Who said that's what I'm doing?"

The Don turned to face him, a stony look in his eyes. "Don't play stupid, Johhny."

"Mock me all you want," Johhny retorted as he stood to leave, "but I remember a time when you would have appreciated my attention to detail."

"Get bent."

"You know, you were the one who made me her handler. But you've become so fucking unpredictable I can't do that job either."

The Don leapt to his feet. "Unpredictable? You know what, Johnny? Go home. Get the fuck out."

Johnny turned and walked out of the office.

"I decide, you hear me?" he shouted after him, flicking his fingers under his chin. "Am I acting like a Don now?"

Massaging the bridge of his nose, he walked to grab a new glass and pour himself another drink.

"Sammy?"

He groaned inwardly. "Yeah, Glo?"

Gloria tapped into the room hesitantly. "What the fuck is wrong with you?"

"Get the fuck outta here, will ya?"

Ignoring him, she closed the door and locked it behind her. "You know what you need?"

"No, Gloria -"

"Nonsense," she snipped, slipping out of her robe. "Come here, have a seat."

Approaching her slowly as he sipped his brandy, the Don watched his wife unbuckle his pants.

"You always think clearer when you've had a nice blowjob," she said matter of factly, giving him a toothy smile.

Sighing and rolling his eyes, he sat in front of her and took another sip.

CHAPTER THIRTY-THREE

Opening the notebook, he turned to the next empty page. Watching the woman cross 17th Street, he clicked his pen and started to write.

"Day two," he muttered, jotting down the notes he'd gathered so far.

There wasn't much to write, though.

Just like yesterday, she left home and drove to a red house in Ybor. And just like yesterday, after a few minutes inside, she left and drove another few minutes up the strip to park behind Margarita's Bar & Grill.

Then, she went home.

Bouncing anxiously in his seat, he tapped his fingers against the steering wheel.

What had he discovered?

She wore black v-necks every day. She looked downright mean — until someone looked at her; then she smiled like Mother Theresa. She gave the same homeless people money today that she had yesterday. She conversed casually with sanitation workers and drag queens alike. She was a nobody and a somebody all the same.

Still, he'd noticed that she was very jumpy. It was almost as if she knew he was watching her.

He sighed. Hoping she had more exciting plans lined up for the day, he went to park his car to await her next move and his next instructions.

CHAPTER THIRTY-FOUR

"Finally."

Tailing the woman for the last week had been some of the most boring work he'd done in his life. But today, she was up to something. Turning slowly onto 17th Street, he dialed a number and pressed send.

"Shit."

She'd turned around and was now staring at him through the windshield, hands on hips. He tried to look away, but she rolled her eyes and approached his window anyway.

"Hey!" she shouted, banging on it twice.

He looked around and covered his face.

"Open the damn window!"

Sighing, he pressed the button and flashed her a smile. "Hey miss lady," he said through a grin. "You just made my day."

"I know you've been following me," she retorted hotly. "What do you want?"

He shook his head and sized her up. "If it ain't obvious…"

"No!" she snapped. "You been looking at me all week. Have some fucking respect."

"I would love to respect you," he said smoothly, trying to calm the situation as he waited for the light to change. "Let me get your number so we can talk about it."

"No!" she snapped again. "I am in *love*. And let me tell you something on behalf of all women. This shit? It ain't fucking sexy!"

"My bad, baby. I been working, I was looking for a chance to talk to you outta my work clothes, you feel me?"

She looked at him thoughtfully. "I been looking for a chance to kick somebody's ass. You feel me?"

"Damn ma, it's like that?"

"Today, tomorrow…it's all the same. If I ever see you again, I will gladly handle that for you."

Watching her march back to 7th Avenue, he asked, "Did you get all that?"

Joe cleared his throat. "Uh, yeah. But what just happened?"

"She made me," Seal explained. "I had to pull the Five Dolla Holla."

"Sounds about right."

Annoyed by the whole situation, Seal asked, "Are you satisfied yet? I'm bored, but also…I'm *pretty sure* that one can kick my ass."

"Pretty sure she can do worse," Joe corrected with a chuckle.

"I believe you. Who is she?"

Joe didn't answer.

"Come on, brother. What's really going on?"

"How did she know she was being followed? I wouldn't have hired you if I didn't think you were the best."

"I am the best," he scoffed. "Now tell me who she is or hang up the -"

Seal laughed when the line went dead.

CHAPTER THIRTY-FIVE

J oe opened the door to his bedroom and waited for Yael to enter before shutting it behind them. Clearing his throat, he tried not to sound as awkward as he had all night.

"Gonna take a shower."

Yael nodded and walked to the window to open the curtains. She turned to give him a small smile, then leaned against the frame to watch the rain.

Joe started the shower, moving quickly. It wasn't that he didn't trust her at all anymore…he just wanted to keep an eye on her.

Scrubbing his body with the loofah he was supposed to have replaced last week, he replayed the scene in his mind. They hadn't slept in the same room in over a month, but he'd run out of excuses tonight. Yael had been asking to have dinner or sit by the water since last month, but his new caseload and her busy schedule made it difficult to work out.

His complaint about their overactive sex life — a painful lie for him to tell — seemed to have worked too well. And even though she swore tonight was just about spending time together, Joe had trouble believing she was really on her period.

Nothing she said was acceptable anymore; he was sure she was lying to him. Of course, he had no definitive proof of anything… but now that he was being honest with himself, he'd admitted Yael was a walking contradiction. The woman was a mixed bag of suspicious behaviors and poor decisions.

Though they still hadn't said 'I love you', hearing it from her lips last week only made his confusion worse. Seeing her visibly pained by his sadness had him diagnosing her with a new psychological issue every damned day. Sure, he blamed the stress on the strain of his caseload — but he could see in her eyes that she knew something *else* was wrong.

Without a doubt, the woman was in love with him. In truth, this was something he still could not understand. Yael was masculine in many of her behaviors, but when it came to him, she was all mushy and lovey dovey. It made no sense. If she truly loved him she would tell him *everything*. Right?

Unfortunately, he didn't know what was true when it came to Yael Phillips. And therein lay his problem.

If Yael really was a psychotic murderer capable of leaving scenes many would have to see to believe, he was happy to have her so close. She was making it easy to catch her. Too easy, though. The woman wasn't stupid, was she?

Common sense said if he had caught her in the act of fleeing the scene that night, she wouldn't keep engaging with the agent in charge of arresting her. But if she didn't know he was a criminal psychologist building a profile against her, what reason would she have to worry?

Rubbing his nether region a bit too roughly with the towel, Joe frowned and took a deep breath. Spending the last month in a frenzy had taken a toll on his mental health; questioning the person he *still* wanted to be with for the rest of his life left him anxious and borderline depressed.

SEAL'S preliminary investigation revealed nothing. She was totally open with Joe about her whereabouts, and Seal found no deviation from the plans and schedules she provided. But the fact that Seal had to dig deeper — needed more time to get to the bottom of things — was all the more suspicious. A few years ago, Yael Phillips didn't even *exist;* that was anything *but* normal.

Swinging open the bathroom door, he found her curled up in the chair in the corner.

"Oh," she said softly, jumping in surprise.

"Sorry," Joe muttered.

Her innocence was also irritating. He hated feeling this way toward her, when she was nothing but loving and sweet to him. But he wasn't a total fool. If she was a *honeypot*, he was already on to her.

Yael stood and stretched, arching her back as she yawned.

Joe turned away, grumbling to himself about how obvious she was being if she was, in fact, a sexy spy.

"Hmm?"

"Didn't say anything."

Ignoring the gloomy look on her face, he pulled up his pants and walked to the window to shut the curtains. He wasn't going to fall into her web again, especially not tonight.

Her hand grasped for his and held it firm, not letting go when he tried to shrug her off. Staring at her pointedly, he tried to show her he wasn't going to bite.

"Talk to me, Joe. Please?"

Mouth tightening, he shook his head. "Time for bed."

"Five minutes? We can just sit and watch the rain?"

He could see her holding back, trying her best to open the line of communication without forcing his hand. She was more patient than he thought she would be, and he hated the situation all the more. Because there was still a chance, that through all of this…she really was innocent.

And if he hurt her then…

"Five minutes," he whispered, avoiding her touch as he moved to sit in the chair.

Spreading his knees wide, he leaned back and relaxed. She clasped her hands together awkwardly and stood in place across from him. Joe knew she would have no choice but to sit on the bed or remain standing, and he only felt a little guilty.

Yael left him lost for words when she leaned down to pull the short footstool from under his seat. She didn't say anything, didn't show any emotion at all, when she slid the stool between his feet. Then, sitting on her hip and folding her legs to the side, she threw her arm over his thigh and rested her chin on her forearm. The touch was a shock to his senses, but her proximity to his groin brought a deep aching from within to the surface.

"Did I do something wrong?"

Joe sat rigidly in the chair and cleared his throat. Pushing his shoulders down to relieve the tension, he gazed up at the ceiling and gave his neck a scratch.

"No," he said, his voice unnervingly flat.

Still staring out the window, she asked, "It really is just about work?"

Nodding, Joe exhaled sharply and closed his eyes.

"So…aren't I supposed to help you?"

"Do what?"

She leaned back into his other leg to face him. "Relax?"

Clearing his throat uncomfortably, he looked out the window and tried to think.

"I've been studying…relationships. And - I," she paused, biting her lip as she chose her words. "I guess I feel like this is my fault."

Staring down at her, his expression hardened. "Really?"

She nodded, not quite meeting his eyes.

He couldn't help but bite. "How so?"

Turning her body forward, she ran her hands up his thighs. "I'm new to this side of things, right? So the way I see it, there are things you need from me that I don't know you need. And you don't know what you don't know, right? So I started looking up all the ways a woman could please a man…and…"

"And?"

Swallowing, she looked into his eyes. "And I think there's something I should do to help you feel…better."

"Better?"

Joe's voice cracked at the same moment his dick began to grow in his pajama pants. He frowned, cursing his body for its betrayal.

But she didn't notice his expression. She was staring, wide eyed and open mouthed, at the tent growing before her eyes. He gave a little squeeze, causing his dick to jump, and couldn't help but laugh when she gasped in surprise.

A brilliant smile crossed her face as she watched him, and Joe felt the guilt flow in. His joy was her joy, always.

"Joe," she whispered, "stand up."

Resisting the urge to point out that a part of him already was, he gave in to her breathless excitement and stood before her. Sitting close as she was, she had to lean back and to the side to avoid being hit in the face by his hardness.

"Joe?"

"Mhm?"

"I want to know what you taste like."

"Jessum peace," he replied, eyes and chin lifting to the ceiling as he exhaled.

She reached up to fold her fingers over his waistband and slid his pants over his hips. Joe looked down, watching her as she examined him up close. He wondered how long she'd be able to keep up the act — if it was an act — before giving herself away. Still, her look of fascination seemed genuine, especially when coupled with her hesitant caresses along his thighs.

"We have to do a test," she said, giving him a smile as she leaned in and planted a kiss on his quad.

Pleasure spread through his body, and Joe instantly remembered why he couldn't possibly let her go. Unless it were some sort of shared psychosis, their kisses were out of this world. Tonight he would learn just how far the magic of this supernatural pleasure went.

"Okay," she whispered, watching him intently. "Now, I'm going to try…here."

The firm, wet kiss she slid along his shaft knocked the wind out of him. Grateful for the safety net the chair beneath him provided, he steadied himself against the wall behind him until he was able to stand on his own.

Yael bit her lip and studied his face. "I see."

Joe grinned.

"I was worried about that," she explained. "But I think we can rectify it like this."

She stuck out her tongue and flicked it across his head, then gave him a questioning look.

Nodding at her, Joe watched as she licked her way up and down his shaft. Her long tongue snaked around him a few more times, but when her lips surrounded his head and she began to suck, he pulled away with a gasp.

Yael frowned. "Does it take a while to get used to?"

"Wha?"

She shrugged. "The feeling, I guess? It wasn't like this in the videos."

Joe's brows shot up. "Videos?"

Yael sucked her teeth and shrugged again. "I told you, I've been studying."

He didn't know what to make of it. He'd told her so many times that what they experienced when they kissed was *not normal*…but she didn't seem to get it. Shaking his head, he gave her a small smile.

"I don't need this, you know?"

Kissing his head softly, she searched his eyes. "What if I do?"

Joe sighed, overwhelmed by the pleasure shooting through him once again. His mind was hazy, which was the last thing he needed right now. He was starting to forget all his questions.

"There's one more thing we can try."

It didn't take Joe long to imagine what she could mean. He scowled. *So she lied about her period after all?*

To his astonishment, Yael opened her mouth wide. Grabbing the base of his dick, she brought her head down to take him in.

"Shit," he moaned, part of him wondering how she expected to explain this.

But the sound of her choking gave him his answer. Yael pulled back and coughed, staring at his dick like it was an optical illusion. "How do they *do* that?"

Joe laughed riotously, shaking his head when she tried again and immediately gagged.

"*Slow down*, sweets."

She beamed up at him and placed a soft kiss just under his head, then stuck her tongue all the way out as she slowly engulfed the first few inches of his rock hard dick. Releasing him when she choked again, she shook her head and threw her hands up.

"I think you should do it."

"Do what?"

Grabbing his hands and placing them on either side of her head, she said, "You do it."

For a moment, he could only stare. But when she gave him a look of impatience, he obliged, poking his head in and out of her mouth as he gently held her in place. She reached up and rubbed his thighs, then tentatively cradled his balls. As usual, he found her apprehensive display as odd as he did stimulating.

Though he tried his best not to push her too far, he could feel Yael leaning in to take more of him into her mouth. After another minute, she grasped his balls more firmly in one hand and wrapped the other around the base of his shaft.

"Yeah," Joe whispered, working hard to control his growing passion.

When she choked again, he stopped and pulled out of her mouth.

"Okay?"

She looked at him and nodded. "I think it makes my mouth wetter?"

"Hmph."

The woman was an enigma. Erotic on accident, and so nonchalant it confused the hell out of him. He had no time to consider what might come next. His head dropped back as she put her hands on his hips and guided him inside. Another minute passed before she stopped again.

"I think I got it," she said, putting her hands on his abs and giving him a push. "Sit."

She giggled when he immediately fell backwards, but a second later she was on her knees before him and holding him firmly in her hands.

"Alright," she whispered, staring at his head with more confidence. "Let's go."

The thought that his lady was a total dork entered and left his mind quickly. All that remained was the feeling of her tongue sliding around the underside of his shaft while she dropped her head down again and again. She was no expert, but her enthusiasm made the experience unbearably arousing.

The kiss she left at the very tip before sliding her tongue down the side caused his eyes to roll back into his head. He thought it was an accident, but one stroke later, he felt her lips again.

Joe looked at her, giving her a smoldering stare.

Eyes darting from side to side in embarrassment, she avoided him; but a few kisses later, she was watching again and didn't look away.

Joe felt the pattern, registering the scale she was building as she worked. A kiss, a lick, then a stroke into her throat. Then, two kisses, a lick on either side, and two deep sucks into her mouth. But just as he thought he had it down, she grabbed his shaft with both hands and rotated in the opposite direction as she sucked away.

He tried to ignore the pattern, but found himself counting anyway, bracing himself for the kiss that never came, or the release of his dick that actually resulted in five extra strokes. And just as he told himself to stop trying to count, she would start a new pattern he couldn't help but catch on to.

Each time he met her eyes, expecting a look of boredom or frustration, he was met with the same zeal and passion she had in the beginning. He wondered when she would give up, but the more he wondered if she would quit him, the more apparent it was she wasn't going to stop. Not until —

Joe exploded, shocking himself as the strangest sense of déjà vu flooded his senses. No one had ever made him come from head alone, but he felt as if he'd lived this moment many times before, felt this exact pleasure on a rainy night he couldn't recall.

He tried to hold back, but she wouldn't allow it. Though the first blast of cum hit her in the lip — causing her some confusion — she recovered quickly.

Yael latched onto his head, squeezed his shaft, and didn't let go. He listened to her moaning, unable to be sure if she was trying to speak or simply enjoying herself. And just when he thought she might finally release him to run to the bathroom, he was awestruck by her empty, open mouth as she licked her way down to his balls. Melting into the chair, all he could do was watch as she licked him softly and intermittently kissed his thighs. She stayed there, nursing him until he was completely flaccid, caressing him with soft brushes of her lips.

Joe sighed and closed his eyes.

To say he was in love was an understatement. There was no way around it. How could he forget that he used to *dream of her*, long before they ever met? How could he ignore the spark between them — the actual, literal electricity that served as a reminder of the magic of their union?

When Yael stood and walked to the bathroom, he could barely keep his eyes open. But his mind was clear now. This relationship had two potential outcomes. The first involved handcuffs; the second involved a ring.

And he knew just the one he'd be paying off tomorrow.

APRIL

CHAPTER THIRTY-SIX

Tommy knocked on the door and took a step back, wondering if anyone was home.

The officer originally assigned to this case was under investigation. Protocol required the rest of his department to pick up the slack. Tommy couldn't quite understand how this was considered the officer's punishment. If he was in charge, he would punish officers by tying them to a desk and giving them everyone else's paperwork. Paid administrative leave should include doing your own paperwork, not passing the buck.

He wasn't surprised, though. He never dreamed of becoming a cop, and even though he'd come to love the work he did in his neighborhood, he couldn't stand the bureaucratic rigamarole. In a few months, he'd be up for review. He had some serious decisions to make about how he wanted to proceed with his career, but for now he intended to ride things out.

Knocking on the door again, he opened his notebook so he could record the visit. A door slammed across the street. Leaning back to check it out, he was surprised to see the bartender walk out of Fred's place.

When he was a kid, he and the neighborhood boys would ride bikes all over — except the road with the red house. Only the most daring boys were willing to ride down this street. Rumor had it the old lady who lived there was not afraid to get a *switch* and tan a few hides. They also said if you complained to your parents they wouldn't care, because her eldest son was capable of putting your daddy in the hospital. If Tommy recalled correctly, the strong man and scary woman were Fred's father and grandmother.

He tried to remember more, but the bartender stopped short when she saw him, eyes wide as she stared into his for a beat. Then she frowned, gave him a curt nod, and continued down the steps.

"Can I help you, officer cop?"

Tommy turned to see the tall woman in the doorway, looking none too pleased to find him there. She was of a sturdy build and the mean mug on her face appeared to be permanent. For a moment, he wondered if *she* was the scary old lady from his childhood. People often moved from house to house around here, so it was a possibility…but no. After giving her the once over, he decided she was too young to be the old lady after all.

Clearing his throat, he did his best to present a respectful tone. "Yes, ma'am. I'm here to speak to Celitha Gordon."

The woman shook her head. "Celitha not here. She at work."

"That's no problem, I can come back…"

When Yael's car rolled past, his eyes followed. He made sure to take a mental note of the make and model as well as the plates.

"Mhm, she been checkin' on the house," the woman offered.

"You know her?"

She nodded. "Mhm, that's Junebug cousin."

"Junebug?" Tommy asked, a puzzled look on his handsome face.

The woman scowled. "Lil' Fred! I know that's what you here for, officer cop."

"Cousin?"

"Mhm," she looked over at the red house across the street. "Thought when she moved in she was one of them lil' hoes he had runnin' through there. But I saw her lookin' just like her momma one day, and I said 'that's the granddaughter!'. She used to come by with her momma — after that I-talian came and took her to a new life. Mhm, I remember…"

Tommy had a feeling he wouldn't need to come back after all.

"Ma'am, if you don't mind, I might be able to take a statement from you?"

Shutting the door behind her, she shuffled her way to a wrought iron chair and sat down. Pointing to the chair on the other side of the mismatched table set, she sat back and began her story.

"That chair got a bad leg, but it should hold you. Celitha not here, she work hard. But I ain't been workin' — on account of my foot — so I seent it all."

"What did you see, miss…Gordon?"

"That's my first husband name. I ain't a Gordon, I'm a Pugh. Edna Pugh."

Tommy wrote her name in his spiral notebook. "Ms. Pugh, I'm here because we have a few different stories of what went on with Fred and Celitha. Now, the statement we received from the case managers says that Celitha had been the one to pick both boys up from karate. Fred says the boys had a good relationship and became close, but Celitha was not a caregiver beyond carpooling and a few sleepovers. What can you tell me about that?"

"Mhm, that's all true."

"Celitha didn't have a larger role in the care of his son?"

Edna gave him the eye. "Like what?"

"I don't know. Did he spend more time here than he did at home? Did Celitha receive any payment? Was she in charge of his welfare?"

"Now what the hell kinda questions is that?" she snapped, a steely frown settling on her face. "They had a good thing going — let me watch my stories in peace. In the mornings, she would drop my grandson off to Fred's house before work. He got the boys fed and got them to school. Then she picked them up from karate since it was on the way from work. That little white boy was a damn racist when he came here, you know. Mhm, he was disrespectful as hell to his daddy."

"What do you mean?"

She looked around, checking if the coast was clear. "Everybody know everybody round here. I seen you before, too, officer cop.

"That little boy think he white — but his daddy *ain't white*. Celitha thought it was a good idea for the boys to play together — they knew each other from school and karate, so it was a nice thing for them to be together after the police brought him from his momma'n'em house."

"I'm sorry. I know their family."

She nodded. "Everybody know they racist, 'specially the old folks. We remember, mhm."

Tommy liked Edna. But her truth wasn't making his job easy. "So, let me make sure I understand. When Fred was granted custody, his son...didn't like him?"

Edna threw her hands up. "Honey, that little boy called his daddy a *nigger* right there cross that street! The whole block heard that boy say it."

Blinking as he wrote, he asked. "With the 'er'?"

Giving him the eye, she nodded. "That's why Celitha ain't mind helping. Fred took over after his daddy passed and he been real good to us."

"Took over?"

Edna thumbed over her shoulder. "I been renting from they family since Celitha was born. She took over the lease last year, but it don't matter no way. I don't think Fred will ever kick us to the curb. He already turned down three of them developers. They wanted this, that, and that whole property, too."

Tommy looked around in awe as she pointed across the street to what he always thought was an abandoned car lot. He'd heard of Frederico — and Fred Sr. — through the years, but he had no idea they owned so much property.

"Alright, I think I'm gonna need your help, Ms. Pugh. When Fred was arrested, the charges included child endangerment and neglect."

"Neglect!"

"Um, yes, ma'am."

"How'd you come up with that?"

Flushed with embarrassment, Tommy was starting to wonder the same thing. "You know, I just got this case. I actually came here to close the investigation, but it looks like there's a lot more missing from the report than I thought."

"Like the truth?"

Tommy sighed, remembering the kind of girl Serafina was. "Ms. Pugh, do you know the mother?"

Edna chuckled. "Child, I know everybody."

"Did you see her the day before Fred was arrested?"

Looking over her shoulder at the lot behind Fred's house, she shook her head. "I knew she was gonna be trouble — her and her little friend."

"Friend?" Tommy flipped through his notes and frowned. "What friend?"

"That little hoe over there — what is her name?" Edna snapped her fingers. "Well, I'd know her if I seen her. And she was barely wearing no clothes! It was too cold out for them little skimpy thangs she had on. Now, the white girl wa'n't supposed to be there at all. He had a 'strainin' order on her, you know?

"Anyway, I was watchin' Criminal Minds and I see her car pull up out the window. I was ready to call the po-lice, honey — she always got something going — but I said, 'let me see first'. She let her friend out and then went to park around back, then she just waited for a while."

"What happened?"

"Her little friend come round the corner and call her over, and then they go inside *together*. I think June called and asked Celitha if the boys could have them a sleepover, 'cause the boy did stay the night. He asked if that was his momma car outside, but we told him it wasn't."

"And how long were they there?"

"I'd say they came round nine or ten. They was still here when I went to bed that evening, but when I woke up 'round fo' the car was gone."

Tommy frowned. "So you didn't see them when they left?"

"Uh uh."

"Did Fred have a lot of visitors?"

"Not since he got his son, officer cop. Now, that cousin of his? Hmm."

"The granddaughter?"

Edna nodded. "Mhm. She been in and out at all hours for as long as I could remember. Sneaky lil' thing."

Resisting the urge to ask more about the bartender who saved his life, he scanned his notes to see what else he might be missing.

"I'm curious," he said thoughtfully. "How were things between Fred and his son just before his arrest?"

"Last times I seen them together, he was hugging him and climbing on him. You know, treating him like a father. It's a real shame what ya'll did to them."

Tommy watched her face contort, the light in her eyes dimming as she slipped into her memory.

"They didn't have to hurt that man — he wasn't fighting them or nothing. Police came and took him, but you just now coming to ask questions?" She stood abruptly, looming over him. "Make a man look like a dog in front his son! Accusing him! Calling him out his name!"

Tommy tried to speak, but she was shouting as she shuffled to the door.

"Don't come back over here, officer cop. And don't be callin' Celitha at work, neither. Shoot you dead myself."

Slamming both the wrought iron screen door and the door to the house, Edna Pugh disappeared in a flash of anger Tommy knew all too well. And if what she said was true, it was likely the rape allegations were also falsified.

Shit.

It didn't help that he was a white cop. And he knew the guys who took Fred in. There was no doubt they'd taken things too far; it was probably the reason said partner was on leave.

And everything happens for a reason...

Tommy's heart sank as he pictured his brother, Matthew, laying in a pool of his own blood. It was the last image he would have of his brother. The pain of that night would be with him forever. It haunted him. And it wasn't the bartender's fault that every time he saw her, he saw Matt. Though she couldn't save his brother, she had saved him.

'*I got him, mister.*'

He shuddered at the bartender's last words to him on that fateful night. Though she was his beautiful guardian angel, she was Matthew's avenger. The parking garage case was still unsolved, but he knew she had fulfilled her promise to end Antoni's life.

Antoni Rizzoli was a racist piece of shit who murdered his brother in cold blood — all because Matt hung out with more black people than he did white.

Antoni's cousin Serafina was a self-proclaimed bitch; he had no doubt she was just as racist as her mother — no matter how many black boyfriends she'd had over the years.

His life had been changed forever by the Rizzoli rage, but it was also saved by the bartender's secret nightlife. Thinking about his brother Matt, he decided that getting to the bottom of this would be the best way to honor his memory.

His sergeant might not approve of the additional investigation, but Captain Johns would. And now, he had a chance to repay the bartender in full.

CHAPTER THIRTY-SEVEN

"I like it. Let's proceed."

"I'll call the notary."

Yael nodded and turned to address Sampson directly. "I need your advice."

"Of course."

"My cousin is being held without bail — and before you make any assumptions, let me explain." She smoothed her skirt, choosing her words carefully. "He's been falsely accused of child abuse, domestic violence, and sexual assault. His accuser was in dependency court and they took her at her word. Based on what I've gathered, she set him up, and the state went right along with it."

"I'm sorry to hear that."

"He's been in jail for almost two months. Obviously, I'm very worried about him. I don't know what I can do for him, other than getting him the best lawyer in the state. I appreciate any recommendations you can provide."

"Yes, madame."

"But more than anything, I'd like to take action against the state, personally. Anyone who has touched his case — including the judge and the lawyer she appointed him — I want their entire career picked apart."

Sampson gave her a curious look, but said nothing.

"Child protective services, too. Oh! *And* the cops who arrested him. They gave him a scar, you know?"

"I'll see what I can do, but…a word of advice?"

Yael lifted a brow.

"The 'state' is a much larger entity than you might imagine. It could be years before you see movement."

"Good thing I have all this money, right?"

If she didn't know the man, she might have misread his smirk. But the glint of humor in his eyes gave her hope that she was starting to grow on him.

"I have a couple cards I can give you today," he said as he rose from behind his desk. "If you'll give me the rest of the week, I should have a more comprehensive list. You're going to need to build a team."

Yael smiled, picturing a group of badass lawyers in suits hopping out of the A-Team van. The team she'd been working with to finalize the dissolution of the Hill trust had done a phenomenal job bringing her up to speed.

She had amassed great wealth in the last six years, and she thought she'd done herself a disservice hiding it away in boxes, storage bins, and attic cabinets. Though it was true she could have doubled it if she invested properly, the recession a few years back would have done some major damage to her finances. Lucky for her, it was now the perfect time to begin her new life as an investor and broker.

Olivier's advice about the property in West Tampa had proven to be sound, and she would soon break ground on a new student housing project for the University of Tampa. She decided to build a mixture of businesses, dormitories, condos, and low-income housing in the same compound — including a grant-funded recreation center for the community to replace the dojo. It wasn't the luxury cash-cow Olivier intended to build, but she had a lot of creative ideas brewing to ensure it was a better fit for the people who already lived there.

At first, it was obvious her team was unsure about her. But once she shared some of her plans and proved she could keep up, they were happy to teach her all about investments and precious commodities. Her extensive collection of hard assets like gold and silver coins and bricks also helped to break the ice.

As for Xavier and Olivier, she was still torn about how to proceed. As long as she was willing to part with a few ancient relics he refused to give up without a fight, she would be able to make a clean break from their loathsome family by the end of the year. And now that today's meeting had finalized the transfer of Xavier's personal wealth and remaining inheritance, she was in the clear as the sole owner of a new estate.

Her estate.

CHAPTER THIRTY-EIGHT

Yael giggled uncontrollably, unable to tear her attention away from the scene unfolding in the center of the bar.

Eileen and Jeanne were reenacting the karaoke show she missed last night — minus the stage, the music, and the talent. The bar was empty for a Wednesday afternoon, but it was still early. Unfortunately for the eight patrons present, the bar had an echo when it was empty.

"And then he was like, 'bay-bay'!" Eileen sang as she posed and pointed to the sky.

Tears rolled down Yael's cheeks as she watched the pair belt out the rest of the lyrics to *Kiss From a Rose*, exaggerating the interpretive moves the couple used while performing the song — three times.

A few other customers chuckled when Yael offered them another round, on the house. Truth be told, she knew the couple in question and had no doubt their show was just as bad as depicted. The regulars in the bar did, too.

"Delivery?"

Yael glanced at the front door and waved them in, smiling and wiping her eyes when the man handed her a clipboard.

"Who are these for?" she asked gleefully, sniffing at the roses another man placed on the counter.

"Miss Peachy?"

Yael frowned. "Is there a card?"

"Yeah," he said, handing her the envelope as he turned to walk back to the door. "Where do you want the rest?"

"The rest?"

They both left before she could get an answer. Opening the envelope and card, her frown deepened with every word she read.

Dearest Peach,

Haven't heard from you, but I shan't give up on our love.

I'll return next season, and things will be different for us.

You deserve to be wooed. You want romance, and I've got plenty.

Goodbye for now, call me anytime.

Olivier

"Girl, you better marry that man!"

Yael shoved the card into her pocket and forced a smile. The delivery driver returned with another vase of long-stemmed roses and gave her an anxious look.

"Just put 'em anywhere," she muttered. "Hey! How many more are there?"

"A lot," he snapped irritably. "Better make room."

Son of a bitch.

"Anybody want some flowers?" She turned and looked at another regular. "Tony? The wife would love these, eh?"

"Fuck no!" Tony shouted back. "Can't have her expecting nice things, can we?"

Eileen and Jeanne rushed over, stopping to smell the roses in each vase.

"I'll take some."

"Me, too!"

Yael smiled broadly at her unofficial best friends. "Next time you sing that song, do it at your own house."

Jeanne looked affronted. "This is my house, kiddo!"

Rolling her eyes at her, Yael watched as the guys brought in another couple of vases. What was she supposed to do with a hundred roses?

"When is the Day of the Dead?"

Tony squinted as he thought. "Ain't that Halloween?"

Damn.

"Cinco de Mayo is next week," she mused aloud. "Maybe we can do something with the two themes?"

Eileen released the vase she and Jeanne were fighting over. "You aren't taking them home?"

"You spinsters take as many as you'd like," she said, giving them a wink. "Red doesn't match my decor."

MAY

CHAPTER THIRTY-NINE

"What do you think?"

Joe faced Weaver and shrugged.

"You haven't said much. All good?"

Nodding, he crossed his arms and turned about the motel room. Weaver stood by and watched, waiting. Joe knew he ought to say something, but his mind was racing. He needed time to think, but time was one thing they didn't have.

"Alright," he offered, trying to find the right words. "It's definitely our guy. But until we hear back from Unit 2, we won't know what happened here."

Clancy poked his head in from the front door. "I just got a text back from Tassel. They're emailing us now."

"Weave, check the file out and find me when you're ready. I'm going to talk to the housekeeper."

Walking out the door and down the long corridor, Joe descended the old cement steps and loosened his tie. It was already hitting ninety degrees in the first week of May, and the humidity felt worse in the middle of state.

Micanopy, Florida was a truck stop town a few exits south of

Gainesville. For decades, signs off I-75 let everyone know the world famous Café Risqué was open for business — and breakfast. The two-star motels on the other side of the highway were the end of the line after a long trip or a long night at the strip club.

Another body in a motel.

It was a familiar scene in Joe's line of work, but it threw a wrench in their entire profile.

The signature was present, but the victim didn't look like a mafioso. And months of what appeared to be an intense escalation were followed by months of silence.

Had he moved on? Was one of their last victims his primary?

Joe didn't know what to think.

If the killer was done in Tampa, they would have to follow the trail of bodies he left in his new territory if they wanted to stop him. If the killer was now moving on to his primary objective, they had no idea how they could warn the final victim.

Mob hits were kept hush hush; most just disappeared, if the victim was even remembered at all. If his serial killer was just that — a hitman for the mafia — that meant anyone connected to the mob could be in danger.

Though he knew the case had been assigned to his special team because of their expertise, he couldn't help but wonder if he was in over his head. There were too many variables at play, and this victim was over a hundred miles away from the killer's playground.

A buzz in his pocket drew his attention. Checking his texts, Weaver's message read: *36 H + mob conx.*

Well, that's something.

Yes, it was. When Joe first saw the photos, he wasn't convinced that this was their case. Still, he knew there were only so many exsanguination cases nationwide at the moment. And though he questioned if it was all a diversion, or even a regression, it might be more simple than anticipated. Running up the steps, he waved Clancy down and found Weaver where he left her.

"Well?"

Clancy spoke up first. "My best guess? Our vic saw his name on a list and ran to paradise."

Joe snorted.

"You know what this means?"

"Don't start," Joe replied, face set firm.

Weaver ignored him. "I'm telling you, there's a war brewing in these streets! These hits are going exactly as planned. Someone is trying to make a statement."

Sighing, Joe raised his brows at Clancy.

"She could be on to something?"

Nodding, Joe conceded. "Alright, Weave. That's your third conspiracy theory about this case."

"And third time's the charm."

Joe gave her a pointed look. "You gonna write it up?"

Weaver blanched. "Uh, no."

"I can ask Tassel?" Clancy volunteered.

Joe put his hands up in protest. "Let's finish here first. We'll revisit the profile in the morning."

"I hope I'm right," Weaver grumbled, following Clancy back to the motel room.

Me too, Joe mused.

If Weaver's latest theory was correct, it would mean they could close the case and be done with this once and for all. Though hitmen and serial killers had a lot in common, the former was only a part of *his* department if they were *also* the latter.

Serial killers fell under his jurisdiction as a criminal psychologist. Joe's specialty was breaking down the mind of a killer. Because hitmen and mob enforcers tended to have a monetary motivation and other factors leading them to kill, his expertise would be unnecessary.

If this was simply a case of a crime family edging someone out, there was nothing to break down, no mystery to be solved. And though Joe had considered that they could be dealing with a rogue enforcer, he also knew that it was more likely the family in question would handle things in-house.

Joe groaned. *That is…if they know he's gone rogue.*

Mob behavior wasn't exactly a major part of his wheelhouse. Tassel would be a great resource, and better still, he wouldn't tip off his superiors just yet. Interdepartmental cooperation could be a challenge between certain units, and Joe had no interest in being stuck working this case with Unit 2. He hoped Tassel could handle a few extra meetings this week. If their guy wasn't a serial, his team needed a clean break.

And so did he, for that matter. After weeks of deliberation, he finally decided to ask Yael to marry him. Last week, he set the plan in motion and requested his birthday weekend off. Things had been better, but he needed to change the energy of their dynamic as soon as possible.

This case wasn't helping in the least bit. A part of him wished he had maintained the tail a bit longer, just so he could confirm Yael hadn't made the drive to Micanopy in the last few days. It was only a few hours, round trip.

After all, who was to say Yael didn't decide to stop killing in Tampa once she ran into him on scene? Actually, it made perfect sense.

If he had been watching her, he would know by now. But since he wasn't…he couldn't help but expect a fiery showdown. The thought of them, standing toe to toe, looking down the barrel of their lover's pistol?

Joe shook his head, forcing the thoughts from his mind. He loved her. He was simply terrified of losing her. But he wouldn't let his fear ruin his happiness anymore.

No more confusion.

Yes. Close the case. Get the girl. Move on. That was all he needed to put this part of his life behind him.

CHAPTER FORTY

J ohhny closed the office door, the thunderous click shaking the stillness of the damp tunnel air. The Don didn't look up from his desk, didn't acknowledge his presence at all.

It had been like that for weeks, the angry tension between them slowly descending into deafening silence. The whole Family was suffering at the hands of the Don, who had gone nuclear after learning of Vitto's intrusion. The kingdom was coming to a standstill, and Johhny had had quite enough.

"What is it?"

He approached the desk slowly, ready to face the music. Whatever happened today, happened.

"I need your approval for a job."

"Oh?" The Don asked, cracking his knuckles when he met his eyes.

Johhny didn't miss the meaning. "Yeah," he said boldly. "She's the best, I need her."

"No."

He tried another angle. "You know Azzo can't resist new pussy. He'll be putty in her hands."

"No," he said flatly, though his eyes bore into Johhny's with a warning to give up.

"Vitto's long gone. Nobody's been able to get ahold of him for months."

The Don slammed his fist onto the desk. "Giuseppe was a one time deal, and you know it. She's not a call girl!"

"Since when?"

"Excuse me?"

Johhny shrugged. "We call, she answers. She don't gotta fuck him, just whack him. What's the big deal?"

The Don rubbed the bridge of his nose. "Why are you doing this, Johhny?"

"My job?"

"Don't play stupid! What are you doing?"

Johhny shook his head. "Nuttin. Just making sure I made the right decision."

"About what?"

He reached over to release the clamp on his wristwatch. Sliding it over his hand, Johhny tossed it onto the desk.

"What are you doing, Johhny?" the Don asked, his voice softening.

"I'm out."

"Out?"

Johhny nodded.

The Don stared at him, an odd look on his face. Johhny waited for the explosion, but it didn't come.

"You'd quit on me, after all these years?"

When he saw the tears in his cousin's eyes, he had to look away. It was the last thing he ever expected to see. Clearing the lump from his throat, he laid it out plain. "You're lying to me. Can't do my job if you're lying to me."

The Don's lips were set firm in a flat line, his nose and eyes turning red under the pressure of his emotion. "Sit down, Johhny."

He took a step back. "I'm serious, Sam."

"Yeah, I know you are. Matter of fact — pour yourself a drink first. Hell, bring the bottle. We're gonna need it."

CHAPTER FORTY-ONE

"I'm just here to talk."

Amber peered out the window then came around to open the door. The look in her eyes was a mixture of shock and disassociation. Tommy was almost certain she was high as a kite.

"Ms. Campbell?"

"Yes, officer?"

"I need you to answer a few questions for me."

Nodding, she joined him outside and closed the door behind her.

"Do you know why I'm here?"

She shook her head, a look of worry crossing her features.

"Ms. Campbell, I'm closing out an investigation and I was told you were a possible eyewitness to a crime reported by Ms. Serafina Rizzoli. Any chance you know what I'm talking about?"

"Uh uh," she said quickly, shaking her head again as her eyes darted around the neighborhood.

"Ms. Rizzoli stated that her son's father drugged her and raped her back in February, but no one has been able to corroborate her story."

Amber took a step back and grasped behind her for the doorknob. "I - I - I don't know nothing about that sir. I see Fi here and there but…"

"Ms. Campbell, you might want to listen to what I have to say," he said quickly, thinking on his feet. "You've been implicated and it could result in some serious charges."

"Charges!" she shouted. "No, no, no. No charges. I didn't do anything!"

Tommy watched her work through her panic, sensing she would crack. He knew it was wrong to lie to her, but…

"Ms. Rizzoli has said otherwise."

"What!"

Feigning a sigh of disappointment, he shook his head. "Her story really doesn't add up, but without your statement there isn't much I can do."

Amber exploded. "Look, sir, I just wanted to fuck Fred, you know? I had a crush on him since, like, the third grade! And she's my homegirl — well, at least I thought she was…so I didn't want to just fuck him, you know?"

"So, you *were* there that day?"

"Yes, but we was high when we got there. And I was awake the whole time. Once she passed out the first time, me and Fred went to the room for a while. Then she woke up and we went to the car to…to get right, you know? And then we stayed the rest of the night."

"So as far you remember, the sex was consensual?"

She nodded. "Honestly, I think Fred was kinda nervous. But Fi was the one who suggested it in the first place."

"Did he give you guys any drugs? Alcohol?"

"No," she replied nervously. "No, we had our own. Fi tried to get him to take some Molly that night but he wouldn't."

"Are you aware that Fred has been locked up for the last three months?"

Amber shook her head, eyes wide. "For real?"

"Ms. Rizzoli didn't mention anything to you?"

"Nah, she went to rehab and now she stay at her momma house mostly. She just come through sometimes to smoke or…yeah…"

Tommy tilted his head to the side. "Didn't you say she went to rehab?"

Amber gave him a smirk. "I know you, sir."

"Huh?"

"I know you from here, officer. Don't make me say it, please? You know what it is."

Sighing, he nodded and closed his notebook. "If you're willing to come with me to the station and give your full sworn statement, you shouldn't face any time for this."

"Sir, I'm high as hell! I can't go to no police station."

"You know me, right?"

She nodded.

"I give you my word. Help me get Fred out of jail, and you and me are good."

CHAPTER FORTY-TWO

Joe straightened his tie in the mirror for the fourth time. Every year he bought himself a new suit on his birthday, but this one was special. This would be the suit he proposed in. Hell, it fit him so nice he was considering getting married in it.

Everything was right on schedule. The restaurant was awaiting their arrival, with their special order in the queue. The small Italian cafe a mile away was Yael's favorite place to dine, but only when it was quiet. Though he had to pay extra — and bribe the night's waiters — they would have their favorite table and those surrounding all to themselves.

Two months ago, when he purchased the ring, he intended to ask her at any moment. All he was waiting for was for her to share something about herself, without prompting. But the longer Fred was in jail, the more detached she had become in their interactions. Though things were actually quite peaceful between them — perfect, really — Joe didn't want to push her knowing what she was dealing with.

And so, time decided that today would be the day. He figured the anniversary of the day they met was special enough, and he intended on starting his proposal by saying the three little words every woman wanted to hear. He wasn't sure Yaya would care, seeing as she never pressured him to say it, and he wasn't afraid to tell her given he'd already heard her own declaration of love.

Smiling at himself in the mirror, he wondered if he would ever get over his suspicions of her. His woman was unlike anyone he'd ever known; he could no longer deny her magic. He'd come to terms with the fact that he was dealing with some sort of mental health issue, and now believed that *any man* with a woman like Yael in their life might find themselves in a similar predicament. Adding in the loss of his wife and son, he was bound to struggle with trusting himself and believing it was safe to love again.

Just as he grabbed his keys and picked up his phone, it buzzed in his hand. Seal was calling. Looking at the clock and realizing he was still extremely early, he picked up and greeted his old friend.

"Where is my gift, brother?"

Seal didn't answer. Then, clearing his throat he said, "Are you sitting down?"

"Don't joke with me, man."

"Shit Joe, I'm serious! Sit down, you need to hear this."

YAEL ARRIVED a few minutes after their reservation, greeting the owner with a big hug and a loud kiss on the cheek. Joe watched her reflection in the glass, waiting for her to join him.

"There's the birthday boy," she said softly in his ear, nuzzling her nose against his neck. "How was your day, handsome?"

Expressionless, he stared down his nose at her when she sat.

"Everything okay?"

He didn't answer her.

"Welcome, bella!"

Yael smiled at their server, a look of confusion on her face.

"Can we have some privacy?" Joe asked coldly.

The server's face lit up. "Of course!"

"What happened?" she whispered, looking around the restaurant.

"I met Philomena."

She leaned away from him as if the weight of hearing her real name knocked her into the back of her seat. Joe watched as she blinked, searching his eyes, but said nothing.

"Philomena Santa Maria Piccirrilo, age twenty three, born January 16th, 1988 to -"

"Stop it."

Joe ignored her, sickened by her tears. "Ran away from home at seventeen after killing her mother in cold blood. Started a new life as Yael Phillips, practiced jiu jitsu at a certain dojo in West Tampa."

Yael wiped a tear from her eye, smearing her mascara down her cheek.

"Is this where you developed your little plot? Is this where I came in?"

A frown formed on her face, but she said nothing.

"I thought so. Now, this is where things get a little confusing. Did you start fucking your instructor, or did your boyfriend convince you to start taking classes? And how is that I came to be your next mark?"

An imperceptible nod led to a face contorted in confusion.

"No? Well," he shook his head bitterly, "I guess it doesn't matter. Tell me — were you there?"

Her eyes widened as he leaned towards her.

"Were you there when he killed them? Was it your idea to leave them for dead?"

Tears burst forth from her eyes as she bit her lips, but still, she did not speak.

He leaned closer and whispered, "You disgust me. To think that you were fucking the man that killed my wife, that you knew and didn't tell me? To think that might not be the worst thing about you?"

She looked at the tablecloth.

"No more tears to cry? You are a sick, sick woman. And you almost had me."

Joe sat back in his chair and glanced around the restaurant. Her lack of response or rebuttal was all the proof he needed.

"I came here tonight because I thought you would be woman enough to admit where you'd been caught." He shrugged. "Every villain reveals their secret plan…nothing you want to say?"

Yael wouldn't look at him, was no longer reacting at all.

"Maybe you are smarter than I'd like to admit?"

When she didn't respond, he pushed himself away from the table.

"I got called in — I've got a flight to catch. I want you gone by the time I return. I'll let the Bureau deal with you later."

CHAPTER FORTY-THREE

Yael felt numb. It was unlikely she would ever feel anything again. Standing in the doorway of her bungalow, she stared blankly at the floor as she tried to motivate herself to get moving. But her tank was empty and she had no idea what would fill it enough for her to survive this.

The range.

Yes, she needed to shoot something. A lot of somethings.

Her feet seemed to move on their own accord, shuffling one in front of the other as she crossed the first floor and climbed the steps. How strange to think this would be the last night she would spend here.

Her legs buckled.

Get a grip!

There was no use crying over spilled milk, right? Joe had just taught her a valuable lesson: she wasn't meant to be happy, to have a companion. She had a job to do, for humanity. There was no happy life for her.

Gazing up the stairway, she pushed herself forward and climbed to the top, avoiding looking out the window at her view of the bay. She had grown fond of her little beach…and her rooftop…

The cockpit, she whined.

She would probably miss her little haven under the sky the most.

Not more than —

Squeezing her eyes shut and shaking her head, she went into her closet to retrieve her range weapons and ammo canister. One year ago to the day, she made plans to go to the range and ended up at Joe's; and to think, she nearly killed him! Now, one year later to the day, here she was making plans to go to the range…

She wondered if Fred would be upset with her if she moved back in. Now that he had lost custody — and since he was still locked up — the threat of Vitto on her tail only affected *her*. All she would need is a few boxes. Her old life was right there waiting for her.

Choking back a sob, she swallowed the bile rising in her throat. Counting to ten as she inhaled and exhaled, Yael changed out of her dress and heels. Once she was back in her standard V-neck and jeans, she tied the laces of her boots and gathered her things.

When would Joe return?

She stared into her closet, eyeing the steps to the cockpit with a heavy sigh. It was best she left tonight, and she knew it.

Range, Wal-Mart for boxes, then…

Dropping her gun case and ammo can on the closet floor, she decided to clear her head for the last time. Climbing the wall ladder, she unlocked the hinges and pushed opened the cockpit door.

Two loud pops startled her, forcing her to jump down or risk a fall.

What the fuck was that?

She was sure they were gunshots — but she was also sure she was seconds away from losing her mind. Staring up at the opening, then looking down at her rifle, she grabbed the handle of the case and leapt to climb into the cockpit.

Unzipping the bag quickly, she pulled the weapon out and dropped the barrel onto the smooth edge of the wooden bowl. Squeezing her left eye shut and staring into the sight with the right, she took a deep, steadying breath. Then, she slid the barrel along, searching for movement. She saw him instantly.

"Vitto," she breathed, watching as he turned from Joe's side door to head her way.

Were they warning shots? Or was his plan to lure her out? Either way, she was grateful Joe wasn't here to witness the unraveling of her entire life.

She didn't have time to think or ask questions. Soon, Vitto would be out of her line of sight. If she didn't do it now, she'd have to face him up close and personal.

Placing her finger on the trigger, she took another deep breath. Then, aiming just ahead of his next step, she squeezed the trigger.

CHAPTER FORTY-FOUR

Yael crossed the lawn on her toes, aiming her Walther toward the spot where Vitto lay dying. She was surprised by the empty feeling that remained, even now. It wasn't that she expected to get over Joe quickly...but this was a much needed victory meant to free her.

Vitto was there, the gunshot to his chest leaving a bloody hole in his shirt. He turned his head as she approached. Gurgling up at her, he lifted a finger and smiled.

Yael gave him a look of disgust, wondering if he was invincible after all. No...he would die. She was certain of it. To kill him now would be too kind.

"Fuck you," she whispered, kneeling down to take his gun.

It was still cold. Checking the magazine, she saw it was loaded.

What the fuck?

Stepping away from him, she aimed her .22 at his head and stared in confusion. He made another sound she was almost sure was laughter.

Yael frowned and surveyed the surrounding the grass. A second gun lay a few yards away. Backing away from him, she stepped towards the weapon and kicked it into the light. If she didn't know any better —

The sound behind her caught her attention. Something was leaking?

Gas?

She frowned and holstered her weapon, wondering if he thought to kill her with an explosion. But when she turned towards the sound, she realized it was water.

It took her a second to make out the figure lying on the ground in the garden. She approached slowly, wondering what she was seeing.

It was his dreadlocks spread about his head that finally helped it click.

Joe.

He was laying there. Facedown. In a muddy pool of his own blood.

She took a step back and felt herself sink into the soft ground just as she heard the *squish*. Vomit rose in her throat. The noise that escaped her sounded inhuman. Then, she saw only red.

Broken, she picked up the gun and ran to stand over Vitto, tripping over her own feet before emptying Joe's clip in the middle of his forehead as she screamed and screamed and screamed.

Yael threw the gun down, raging as she felt her whole world crashing around her. Where before she felt nothing, now she felt…*everything*. Dropping to her knees, unable to stand, she cried her heart out until she had nothing left.

Run.

She heard it in the back of her mind, a still small voice she did not recognize.

Run!

Yael tried to stand, but fell, sobbing all the more.

Run damn it! Run! Run!

She was on her knees, dragging herself away from the horror she had caused. A few yards later, she made it onto her feet.

Rounding the corner to her driveway, she stopped short of the front steps, staring down at her shoes as she cried silent tears. She tore at the strings of her boots and kicked them off, unable to bear the sight of the man's blood on the pristine marble flooring within.

Sprinting to the stairs, she slid into the wall with a loud thud, then scrambled up the steps. Where would she go now? Now that she had killed them both?

In her closet, she located her go-bag and stared up at the open cockpit. If only she had climbed up sooner. If only she had tried to explain herself at dinner.

If only...

Shaking the thoughts from her mind, she slapped herself twice in the cheek.

"Think!" she shouted, slapping herself again, harder.

But nothing came. Because deep down, she knew, she had no one.

The sobs returned, this time mingling with the screams of a woman who lost her soul. She tore at her clothes in the closet, destroying everything she could reach.

The card that fell to the floor made it into her hand. But just as she went to tear it to pieces, she saw the phone number.

No.

"Yes," she whispered.

No!

She crawled out of the closet, searching for her cell.

Don't!

Dialing the number with shaking hands, she held the receiver to her ear and listened as the phone rang.

Hang up! Hang up the fucking phone!

"Hello? I'm ready."

DECEMBER

Ybor City, Florida | 1986

"See you tomorrow, Mr. Scavo!"

Startled, Andrea nearly dropped the glass he was shining. His face was ashen.

"Mr. Scavo?"

Andrea placed the glass down with trembling hands, steadying himself on the counter. Then, he grasped to his left at the vase full of change and singles and fished out a wad of cash.

"You alright? You don't look too good, sir."

"You're a good boy," he finally whispered in reply, clutching the bar as he approached. "Here, take it."

"Mr. Scavo! I couldn't take this, it's too much!"

The old man was shaking, but said nothing as he walked him to the back door and ushered him outside.

"Be safe tonight, *passerotto*."

The crack in his voice was troubling, but there was no time to respond. Andrea Scavo slammed the door to the employee entrance of L'Unione Italiana and locked it soundly.

Counting the crumpled bills in his hand in the dim light of the bulb over the door, he was surprised to find a hundred dollar bill between two singles. The last few years of working at the restaurant after board meetings and events had been good to him, and he'd even been handed a few larger bills in that time. But *this* was tip money from behind the bar, and there was no way Mr. Scavo intended for him to have it. As stoked as he was to see it, he didn't want to put the old man in a bad spot. He turned and knocked on the door.

"Hey! Mr. Scavo?"

The light turned off above him. He banged again.

"What'd you win the lottery or something?"

No answer. Andrea had been twitchy all night, and this was the icing on the cake.

Shaking his head and pocketing the money, he decided to return the extra hundred the following day after school when the club was open. If he didn't, his mother would never let him live it down.

The back lot lost more light when an upstairs window went dark. Apparently, Mr. Scavo was trying to send him on his way.

"I give," he muttered, eyeing the upper windows in exasperation. Readjusting his school satchel, he tucked his hands into his jacket pockets and started into the darkness.

Ybor City was silent tonight. The week after Thanksgiving was usually a quiet time as the neighborhood geared up for Christmas celebrations and merriment. By mid-month, the city would be alive almost twenty-four hours a day. Sadly, on this nippy Florida evening, there would be no ride home.

Not that it mattered. Even without the extra money, he finally made enough to buy his lady love the stationery she had her eye on over at Woolworths. It was the most expensive thing he would purchase in his eighteen years to date and he would do it all over again…for her.

A black Pontiac sedan drove into the lot and headed straight for him. He froze, mouth agape in the headlights, snapping out of it when the lights flashed bright and then turned off.

"Geez," he sighed out, squeezing his eyes shut against the temporary blindness.

Were they here to give him a ride home? Mr. Scavo's old BMW was parked at the end of the lot, but maybe he was having car trouble?

"Look who we have here…"

He froze again. He knew that voice all too well. Turning slowly to face the car, he watched as all four doors opened in unison. Frankie Scaramucci and his gang made quick work of surrounding him. The first punch landed hard.

"What's a *good boy* like you doing out so late?"

Another punch to the face sent him reeling, but two strong arms on either side kept him on his feet. A third punch to the gut knocked the wind out of him.

"You think you can just go around breaking hearts and nobody's gonna have a problem?"

Silvia?

He could barely think straight as another fist came flying at the bridge of his nose.

"*Papa* has a message for you."

"For the whole neighborhood," another voice piped up.

"Yeah, and the message is real simple. Nobody crosses a Rizzoli and gets away with it. Not even *Mr. Perfect.*"

"College boy isn't gonna look like such a *wiz* in the morning, is he?"

"College boy isn't gonna *see* morning," Frankie retorted, a broad smile spreading across his face.

The whole crew laughed as Frankie delivered an uppercut with a flourish.

"I thought we was gonna take our time with this one?"

Frankie took a step back and threw his hands up. "Go ahead! Just remember, wiz kid's mine. Fucking moolie lover!"

The kick to his chest was unexpected. The guys holding him up dropped him as he crumbled, wheezing, unable to find his breath.

Am I dying?

He wasn't sure, but all he could wish for now was a swift death. Rumors were swirling that Papa Rizzoli had gone off the rails. Women and children were no longer off limits, but men? Closed casket funerals had become the norm the last few years. What were they planning on doing to him? This couldn't be the beginning, just the start of his torture?

No.

He knew there was no way out, no way he would survive a mafia hit. But maybe he could end this now.

"Fuck you," he spat out.

"What the fuck did you just say to me?"

"I curse you," he gasped, pointing a shaking finger at them all. "You, and you."

The young men gawked at him, eyes wide with fear. He stared boldly at Frankie.

"And you? I curse your *mother*."

Frankie growled and lunged for him. The sound of the car door slamming behind them seemed to startle him and he fell to the ground.

Though it pained him to do so, he turned his head to face Frankie. He wouldn't go out like a coward, even if he was about to have his brains beat in. To his surprise, Frankie was staring back at him with a blank look on his face.

"Shit!"

The car door slammed again. He heard another loud thud.

"Carlo? No!"

He tried to sit up to see who was in the car, but his body wouldn't cooperate. Blackness began to overtake him when he heard another door slam. A sudden weight on his ankle almost broke it, but the pain brought him back to his senses and gave him the rush he needed to pull himself up off the pavement.

The car doors were all shut. Frankie lay next to him, unmoving, and Carlo was splayed out across from him; he recognized it was Carlo's cousin Tommaso who had landed on his leg. Only Alessio remained standing, his eyes on the woman just beyond the car.

Though he saw her there, and recognized the look of shock in her eyes as she stared into his, he couldn't quite comprehend what was happening. Was any of this real? Or had he already died and gone to heaven?

"Stef?!"

His heart dropped into his stomach when Alessio leaped toward her.

She gasped.

The car door slammed again.

Alessio collapsed.

Blinking, his eyes flitted back and forth, finally landing on the metal shining in her gloved hands. He stared at it, his vision going in and out, until he realized what he was seeing.

A gun?

Unable to speak, he stared into her eyes, tears forming in his own.

She raced around the car, a sob escaping her as she tripped over Tommaso and slid onto her knees. Her fingertips stopped just short of his face; then she followed his eyes to the gun in her other hand.

"What happened here?" she asked, holstering the gun and looking at the fallen men.

Try as he might, he couldn't figure out where to start. And to think *she* was the one asking questions! "Where'd you get a gun?"

"Can you walk?"

"And why do you have a *silencer*?" he questioned harshly.

"We have to go!" she snapped. "Can you walk, or not?

Rising to stand over him, she put her hands on her hips and glanced around.

He felt his eye swelling, and he could swear they cracked his ribs; but the dead weight on his ankle needed to be removed for him to assess the damage.

As if reading his mind, she moved toward Tommaso and kicked him in the head. When he didn't move, she squatted down and started picking his pockets.

"What the hell are you doing? Get him off me!"

"Gotta make it look like a robbery," she said in a quaking voice as she slid the watch off of Tommaso's wrist. She pocketed the cash in his wallet and threw it aside, then went for the clasp of his gold chain.

"How did you know I'd be working late?"

"I didn't."

She rolled Tommaso off his leg with a push, then turned to face him. There was a hardness there he had never seen before.

He frowned, watching her move to Carlo's pockets as she used her wrist to wipe a fresh tear from her cheek. She shot him a glance.

"Are you gonna tell me what happened here?"

He shook his head.

She scowled, then shrugged and lifted her chin pridefully as she moved to check Alessio.

Surveying the lot, he wondered if anyone could see them. From where he sat, the car was cover enough in the darkness. The night's new moon provided no light.

He knew he ought to tell her. A hit-gone-wrong would not be the end of this.

Clearing his throat, all he could say was, "*Papa* sent 'em."

She whirled around to face him.

"Payback for Silvia," he confirmed.

She gasped. "Tell me you lie?"

He shook his head. When her face began to contort, he bit his lip; new tears formed in his eyes. Grunting, he rolled onto his side and busied himself with Frankie's watch.

Joining him, she knelt and went for Frankie's chain, sniffling through the tears.

"What were you doing out so late, *bellezza*?"

Even with his softened tone, she wouldn't answer.

"Come on?" he whispered. "I told you mine, now tell me yours."

Leaning to scoop up his bag and throw it over her shoulder, she didn't say a word.

"Geez! If I'm gonna die for you, at least tell me something!"

"No!" she screamed. "You're *not* gonna die!"

"I almost did! Tell me how I'm still here? How did you know to come here?"

"We have to go!"

She tried to yank him to his feet, but wavered in her effort. Then, the floodgates opened and her sobs flowed forth.

He pulled her onto his lap and wrapped her in his arms, holding her knowingly as she began to break down. Staring at the bodies surrounding them, he rocked her back and forth, ignoring his own physical pain, mental anguish, and the feeling of terror creeping up his spine.

"*'Voi che per li occhi mi passaste'l core'...*"

She took a deep breath, wiped her eyes and raised her chin to meet his lips. Kissing him softly, she rested her hand on his cheek and sighed. Taking another breath, she replied.

"*'L'amor che move il sole e l'altre stelle.'*"

"Tell me you trust me, *amore*?"

Without hesitation, she nodded and kissed him again, caressing his cheek when he winced.

"And I can trust you?"

She sighed. "Can you walk?"

"You -"

She put a finger to his lips.

"I think I know how to fix this. And if you can get up…I'll tell you everything."

Made in United States
Orlando, FL
08 June 2022